I0522520

I wanted love and a daughter, but it was a lot harder getting them than I had thought…

I opened the card, hoping it was from Josh. They were from Milt, begging my forgiveness. I scribbled a note, *I don't want to see or hear from you right now. Don't push me or we leave today*, and handed it to the girl. "Please deliver this to the man who sent this stuff. The front desk will know where he is."

He never hit me again, but he raged often. Almost all of his outbursts were the result of me pushing his buttons. One of my bad qualities was detecting men's vulnerabilities and poking them in their weak spots. Maybe I had a sadomasochistic streak. Other men had reacted negatively, but they didn't hit me. Milt wasn't violent unless I provoked him. It was my fault, but I no longer cared.

Milt knew to keep his distance and met me for lunch at the maître d's stand.

"We'd like a quiet table in the corner."

The maître d' motioned us to follow him. "This way."

As soon as we placed or orders, Milt started in. "I really can't bear—"

"Can it, Milt. This is how it's gonna be." *I can't stand being near you anymore.*

Mothering her brothers wasn't enough, Tookie wants a child of her own. After "auditioning" numerous men—one date at a time—all of them fail the test. Frantic, with her biological clock ticking down, she accepts a blind date with momma's-boy engineer, Ollie, who works with her secretary's husband. Ollie's old-country mother, Rose, yearns for grandchildren, but will she squash Tookie when her PI uncovers Tookie's past indiscretions?

Regan Murphy, The Review Team of Taylor Jones &
Regan Murphy

ACKNOWLEDGMENTS

The Critters at CritiqueCircle.com aided me immensely by gently (usually) but firmly advising me where improvements were needed by slogging through my book chapter by chapter week by week. Special thanks go to Black Opal Books' artist Jack for bearing with me during the search for cover art.

FINDING MR. WRONG

GEORGE KAPLAN

A Black Opal Books Publication

Finding Mr. Wrong

Prologue

My First Cruise

1977:

With a little help from the pharmaceutical industry, I got over the seasickness I suffered on the Windjammer cruise with the girls from my office at Carver-Watkins. They shocked me, then an innocent eighteen-year-old virgin, with their rough language and wild ways when I first started to work there nine years ago. After declining timid Tim's proposal and splitting with him, I adopted some of their behavior, opening a whole new world of experiences to me. I was always on the periphery of this clique, more so now that I was a member of professional staff, but they needed another person to make the trip work financially. Having vacation days to use or lose tipped the scales in favor of going on this adventure.

Wearing a swimming suit onboard put me at a severe disadvantage in attracting the youngish crew. Falsies were out of the question because I wasn't about to risk having foam rubber cones float up to the surface if I fell overboard. My body and a passenger list that excluded men conspired to protect me from my extremely vulnerable self. Expecting to be melancholic at the least without a boyfriend or prospects for a shipboard romance, a surprisingly high seventy-five happiness quotient for this semen-free vacation indicated that I had enjoyed this escape more than recent penis-enhanced ones. Even without an opportunity for sperm infusions, the trip proved to be a therapeutic getaway that rejuvenated me.

Professional women in the statistics department hadn't fully accepted me, possibly because I'd worked my way through college and only had my degree for a year. They weren't used to thinking of me as an equal, even though I graduated magna cum laude. And my former cohorts, the girls in the clerical pool, had distanced themselves since I'd been promoted. Evenings on the cruise gave them and me time to rebound by sharing tales about boyfriends and lovers. One night on the deck under the stars became particularly memorable when excessive alcohol intake overcame inhibitions and loosened tongues.

"Too bad about Isaac, Tookie," said snake-tongued Jackie. "You won't be his last."

"Please. He's history now. I'm done with him." *Is nothing secret in our office?*

"Got somebody else in mind?" slurred dirty-minded Cheryl, the typist for my new department.

"Not a soul." First boyfriend Tim was too conventional, but I could talk him into seeing me again if I wanted.

Cheryl spoke with a lopsided grin. "Any of you been to Eve's Garden?"

Most had blank looks on their faces.

"You mean that sex shop in the city that was in the papers a couple of years ago?" Jackie would have been there the day it opened, but she'd never admit it.

"They have these things there that, uh, uh, you could use when you don't have a man in your life." Cheryl twinkled, as if just thinking about it was bringing her to orgasm. Her nipples looked like the tips of Atlas rockets trying to launch through her bikini top. I expected to see her hand in her crotch any second.

Jackie teased. "So that's why you're always disappearing into the john."

Cheryl rolled her eyes and turned to address me. "They even have classes to show you how to use them. Wanna sign up for one with me when we get back?"

This sounded promising. "Is that the place where teacher hands out vibrators to a dozen naked women then shows them how to use them to get off?"

"No, that's some other place," insisted Cheryl. "This place is classy."

"No thanks. I prefer the real thing." *Better check this place out as soon as we get back.*

With my system flushed from the recent past, I returned to work feeling revitalized. However, the first few days back weren't without their moments.

The first time I encountered Isaac in a deserted hallway, he tried to pass me without speaking.

"Can't you look at me, you bastard?" I blocked his path, thinking he wouldn't push me out of his way. He was a son of a bitch but not a brute.

"Let me by, please?" he asked, looking down, avoiding eye contact.

"You tell me how deeply you love me then move out without a word."

Still looking down, he said, "You don't understand."

"Understand what? You ask for—and get—a world-class blow job, then you fuck me stupid the rest of the night, all the while knowing you're going back to your wife as soon as I leave for work. Is this how you show undying love?"

He reached out to touch me.

I slapped his hands away as hard as I could. "Don't you dare."

He lifted his head, but not high enough for me to see his face. "She threatened to clean me out if I didn't."

"So, your love has a price tag." My temperature rose with each lie.

"I'd lose everything, and I'm too old to start over." He pleaded as if asking for forgiveness.

"You fucking liar. That isn't what you said before you begged me to suck your puny pud the last time."

"We're soulmates, and I don't want to lose you." *What a great line. I hope to use it myself.*

"Soul fucking mates is more like it." My anger rose exponentially after his last lie.

"We can still see each other. She left on a business trip this morning."

I kneed him in the balls, something I'd fantasized about doing to various men who'd wronged me but never had the opportunity and the courage at the same time before.

"Ooohhh," he moaned as he fell to the floor, grimacing in pain with his hands protecting his groin from further attack.

"Don't you ever talk to me again. I no longer exist as far as you're concerned." I strutted away very proud of myself for finally giving a man what he had coming.

Rumors circulated around the office after Isaac was found lying on the carpet groaning and holding his family jewels. No lie he could make up was believable. It was obvious he'd taken a punch, kick or knee to where it hurt most. Everyone knew I had the motive, but no one thought I had the strength or audacity to deliver such a blow. It remained a Carver-Watkins mystery.

❧❧❧

I was ready for a new relationship. But who? I'd already schtupped all the guys in the office with functioning equipment and a few whose weren't. I had to look elsewhere.

Finding a new lover wasn't easy for me because I'm basically shy. I could play a role for a few hours on one-night stands when I wasn't looking for a relationship. Acting easy got me sex with handsome guys who wouldn't consider dating me. Oh, how some of them slapped my beaver. They'd had lots of practice. Beautiful girls threw themselves at these guys, but they seldom bothered to learn how to please a man. They expected men to please them. This was my advantage.

I knew how to, and often did, give these guys the mind-blowing sex they didn't get from gorgeous girls. I got off seeing the shocked looks on these guy's faces when I took charge. Some of them wanted to date me afterward, but an ego boost was enough for me. Relationships with these guys wouldn't work. Any guy I dated had to be able to carry on an intelligent conversation.

With no Mr. Right waiting for me on the dock or at the office, I made a beeline to Eve's Garden. She let me test drive Prelude, the Panabrator and the Magic Wand with differing results. Prelude looked like a gun and had nasty little attachments. Its silent operation was a plus, but it quickly got too hot to hold. The Panabrator was loud. It sounded like a diesel truck in low gear. No chance of jilling out undetected with it, but it was great at getting me over the mountain. The Magic Wand, or Big Buzzy as some women called him, gave my clit all she wanted and more. I dubbed the one I bought "Sydney."

Maybe I could open up an Underwriters Lab sort of thing to field test these babies. Now that would be a dream job.

Reassessing my "No Props" rule hurt my ego, but I've never regretted having him at my bedside. He's never broken a date, farted in bed, or hurt my feelings. My ideal would be highly intelligent, handsome, sensitive to my needs, and able to please me as well as Sydney. He would make his first priority plowing my furrow deep and planting his seed nonstop until my daughter grew inside me. Where could I find such a man?

CHAPTER 1

Jack

That's the best book on the subject, and it costs a dollar less than the others," drawled the soft baritone voice that interrupted my browsing of a dog training book.

Facing the bookshelf with my nearsighted eyes buried in the oversized paperback, I couldn't see who made what could only be a sales pitch or a come-on line. I hoped for the latter. Wanting to see what he looked like before I responded, I looked to my right as far as my peripheral vision allowed. All I could see was the leather elbow patch on the left sleeve of his well-worn green corduroy jacket. Wondering what life would be like married to a southern literary type, I straightened up and turned to get a better look.

Trim, not overly tall, auburn hair graying at the temples, the mystery man looked how I imagined an author might look. The way his eyes scanned me from head to tail told me it wasn't a book he was trying to sell me. I decided to act coy even though dating an author was high on my before-matrimony list, the adventures I wanted to have before settling down.

"Says who?" I said, turning to get a good look at him.

"The publisher." His sly smile told me he liked my front, from the shoulders up anyway, as well as my bottom.

"And who'd that be?" I turned the book over and looked at the flap on the off chance he was the author. He wasn't.

"Me."

"You? Get serious."

He didn't look like what I expected a publisher to look like. For starters, he wasn't chewing a cigar.

"The company I work for, actually."

Seeing the name on the book's spine, I parried, "Emerald Isle Publishing? Never heard of them."

"He's not one of the authors I work with personally."

"Who do you work with?"

He straightened up as if the next thing he was going to say was important. "Lance Lattrell."

"The mystery writer?" Okay, he was getting more interesting.

"He's giving a talk in this very store today." His smile disarmed me.

"Where? I read his books all the time," I lied. I'd read part of one, though, but didn't like it.

"Over there." He pointed toward a podium in the far corner of the store. "Coffee?"

He seemed to be interested. I couldn't act too eager. "Don't drink it."

"I'll buy you a beverage of your choice—tea, cocoa, soft drink, water…"

"I don't think I have time." Having only forty hours to fill before getting up for work Monday morning, I looked at my watch.

"One cup won't take long, Red."

"The name's Mary Louise, but most call me Tookie."

"Jack. Not John. Just Jack. What's your poison?" His smile broadened in what must have been another attempt to penetrate my defenses.

"Cranberry juice. But just in the store, not out any-where." I was much safer here. For all I knew, he was the Ramsey Rapist the homicide squad was trying to catch.

Prowling The Happy Booker, my favorite local bookstore, during peak pickup hours and on weekend af-ternoons had netted me much mediocre sex with men I didn't want to date. My incorrigible optimism led me there during dating gaps. However, I'd never go near the place on a weekend night. Hanging out there then would advertise my datelessness to ultra-nerdy guys who hit on me all too often as it was.

The Happy Booker was the first bookstore in my ar-ea with a small café and couches placed invitingly among the shelves. I tried loitering in various sections, but pets seemed to attract men who shared my interest in dogs. Someday, I'd have one, a golden retriever or yellow lab.

Before leaving Jack's hotel room after room-service breakfast the next morning, he asked me out to dinner.

Jack stayed in the hotel to be close by if Lance needed anything and to chauffeur him around to his talks. I temporarily put my objective to date an author on hold—an associate publisher would have to do for the time being. Sharing his bed might eventually lead me to authors. If I was extremely lucky, Jack might turn out to be Mr. Right.

⌘⌘

I've always been an avid reader but knew nothing about what it took to get a book from an idea to printing several thousand copies. Jack taught me the fundamentals of the trade, and I treated him to a few tricks from my broad repertoire. Jack listened to me over dinner and other times when I kvetched about friends, family, coworkers, and bosses, something only Tim had ever tolerated. He didn't rush me into bed, always taking me on proper dates first. The major downside to dating him was his frequent out-of-town book signing trips with authors. I was thrilled when, over a rare weeknight dinner, he invited me to accompany him to a trade show after having spent several weekends home alone with Sydney in recent months.

"What'll I have to do?" I'd never worked a trade show of any type before, but he didn't need to know that. If things didn't work out with Jack, I might meet my author there.

"Not much. You'll handle the overflow the few times I'm busy, and you'll model the leading lady from the new book we're promoting."

I reached across the table to pick up the hardback novel Jack brought with him. "Hey. She looks kinda like me but sexy." Noticing the Tommy gun on the cover, I asked, "Is she his moll?"

"Read the chapters I've marked, so you'll know what kind of mannerisms you'll need."

Although skeptical of what he was up to, I didn't want to spend another weekend alone, especially when we could be doing the horizontal mambo in a five-star hotel. And it might just move him to start our family.

"Great news!" I reported over the phone after buying sexy lingerie instead of eating lunch the next day. "They'll let me off work to go with you, and I'll only have to burn two vacation days."

"Don't forget you're my assistant, and you've got to follow orders at the show." His tone undercut his otherwise affectionate demeanor.

"Have you made an appointment to get unfixed as soon as we get back?" Prior to this, he'd balked at even talking about impregnating me.

"Is that your price for doing whatever I ask in Atlanta?" He looked more serious than I'd ever seen him.

"You could look at it that way." My price was a ticket for the baby train sometime in the future.

✵✵✵

We flew first-class to Atlanta, where we stayed in the most luxurious hotel I'd ever been in on a tryst. How great was that? I was the one being pampered for a change. After bouncing on the comfy bed, I poked my head into the closet, where an unpleasant surprise awaited me.

"What's *this*?" I picked up the sexy dress with two fingers and tossed it on the bed.

"It's for you to wear in the booth," he said with a straight face.

I'd never worn a dress with fringe or sparkles before and didn't intend to wear one then. I shuddered to think why he wanted me to wear something so flashy. Tim never did anything like this to me. He loved me too much. "No way."

"Way. They won't pay you or your travel expenses if you don't." He didn't waver.

Jack handed me the emerald green flapper-style dress in exactly the right size (which I won't divulge) and in a beautiful color perfect for me. The length was ideal. It covered my not especially photogenic knees while shifting attention from my chest to my rear. I seldom wore dresses, let alone anything stylish. This one wasn't revealing, just showy. Too showy for me.

"Try it on." Jack opened a dresser drawer and pulled out a flat Frederick's bag. "I think the sizes are right," he said, handing it to me. "And put the slip on first. It'll make the dress shimmy more."

Inside the bag was a sexy black garter belt I'd model in the boudoir, but I had no intention of hanging nylons from it. "The sizes don't matter. I'm not wearing them."

"You can't go barelegged," he barked. "They're better than panty hose."

"I thought I was working a book fair and you've sold me to a brothel."

"Tookie!" I'd never heard him raise his voice before. "Besides, I think you'd look even sexier in stockings with seams." He failed to hide his devious smile.

"You wear them, then." If thoughts had power, his balls would have shriveled to the size of peanuts.

"Put them on or go home. Boss's order." Jack was downright belligerent. He handed me one of them to put on and waited for me to roll it up my leg before giving me the other one.

I reached my hand out to him. "Give it to me and leave the room. Can't a lady have a little privacy when she's dressing?"

"When did you start wanting privacy?"

Checkmate. Damn him. He'd outmaneuvered me. I shouldn't have asked him to have sex in the picture window.

Aligning the seams on the backs of my legs so they were perfectly straight was a royal pain in the ass. The beaded flapper slid back and forth against the silk slip, and the fringe tickled my knees.

"Look," he said, turning me to face the mirror.

"That can't be me. I look…stunning." The style and cut of the dress accentuated my assets and camouflaged my deficiencies. The color contrasted my hair like nothing I'd worn before or since. It even brought out my green eyes. I looked beautiful for the first time in my life. But, still, I was just not a glamorous person and didn't feel comfortable masquerading as one. In the mirror, I saw movement in Jack's trousers. His penis thought I looked sexy in the outfit, but it'd have to wait until I was ready for a snack.

"Not now. When it comes off, it's staying off. Let's get this over with."

In the elevator, he refreshed me about "Jessica," the protagonist's squeeze I was playing that day from their new, what they hoped would be, bestseller.

"Jessica's a rabbminx—"

"What's that?"

"A woman who copulates with the frequency of a rabbit and the skill and enthusiasm of a minx."

"I always try to do my best. This why you picked me?"

He hesitated. "After reading the manuscript, I had the artist model the cover image after you."

"I see you hold me in high esteem."

"She's also a flashy dresser, the girlfriend of a John Dillinger-like character."

"So, I'm playing a gun-moll flapper whore." *You better start treating me better and soon.*

"I wouldn't put it that way."

"Sure."

Men ogled me. Some even whistled as I made the long walk from the elevator down the long corridor to the exhibit hall. The fringe swung with each step. When I shook my fanny the least bit, the beaded strings swayed from side to side, exaggerating my every movement and generating even more attention, most of it unwanted.

Aside from having to stand in heels all day and dealing with a few gold-plated jerks, I enjoyed working that show.

Since only booksellers were admitted, publishers lavished attendees with free copies of new releases to consider stocking in their stores. I kept busy replenishing the shelves in Jack's booth.

Only occasionally did I talk with potential customers. I hadn't been prepped to do this, but I was smart enough to make up what sounded like good answers to their questions.

Playing a character so different from myself gave me more confidence when I did it well. I improvised and tried out various aspects of Jessica on and off the exhibit floor. Modesty keeps me from saying how fantastic I was.

Every time I was alone in the booth or when Jack huddled with a potential customer, horny jerks approached me and made dreadful passes. One of these horndogs was particularly obnoxious.

"When do you go on break, honey?" came gruffly to my ear as I felt a giant-size meat hook fondle my ass.

I turned to see a two-bit man in a five-hundred-dollar suit holding a fistful of Franklins and a lascivious look on his face.

"I'll make it worth your while," said the sixtyish lecher with bad skin and a banana for brains.

Thwack! I slapped him—hard. Jack couldn't help but hear the pop it made and gave me a sideways glance. I saw his tiny grin. *Bastard. You set me up for this.*

禄

Back in the room hungry after what I'd been through that day, I asked, "What's for dinner?"

"You."

"In your dreams. Get up and get dressed."

"Wear what you wore today." He licked his lips lustfully. "I'll even take you dancing."

"When's your appointment?" I smelled a rat.

He looked past me. "I haven't made one."

"You promised." He'd never give me my daughter shooting blanks.

"I thought you'd renege on the dress."

"You lying bastard. So, you never intended to get your vasectomy reversed, you scumbag."

"I'm not undoing it."

"Why do I always fall for assholes? I'm getting out of here. Don't expect any more from me. Ever."

I retreated into the bathroom and turned on the shower so he couldn't see or hear me cry. He didn't care about me. I did everything he asked, and he broke his promise. I never felt so used.

The shower calmed me enough to think straight. I dried off and fluffed my hair, so I looked considerably better than I felt. I wrapped a towel around me and opened the door.

"Took—"

"See these lips?" I pointed to my mouth. "See this tongue?" I stuck it out as far as I could and pointed it at him. "They've licked and sucked your pathetic pecker for the last time." I dropped the towel, spread my legs, and pointed to my cockpit with both hands, stewardess style.

"See this cunt? Get a good look. You're never seeing it, let alone fucking it, again."

"But I—" He put his arm around me. I flicked it away as if he was a cockroach.

"Don't touch me. All I am to you is a hole to stick your blank-shooting dingaling in."

"That's not fair. You don't want to get pregnant."

"Someday I will." And that day was getting closer all the time.

I threw on some clothes and stuffed the rest, including the green dress, into my suitcase, and ran out the door. I raced out of the elevator on the Concierge Floor, into the room the company used as a hospitality suite during the day, and locked the door behind me. That night, I cried myself to sleep. Early at the airport, feeling cheap and used, I changed my seat assignment for the flight home to sit as far from him as I could—without leaving first-class.

The next guy would treat me better, and I'd make sure he was capable of giving me a baby from the get-go.

CHAPTER 2

Ken

A letter from the county court system was the only non-junk in my mailbox when I returned to my lonely apartment from the ill-fated weekend in Atlanta with blank-shooting liar Jack. I thought it might be cool, especially if I got a murder case. Boyfriendless, I focused my time and efforts in the man-desert I called work to pass the days and position myself better for a possible promotion.

After two weeks of diligence, I found myself biding my time in the jury room reading *A Demon in My View*. A bailiff or guard or some guy like that wearing a gun caught my attention when he walked past me on his way to the front of the room.

My nipples picked a lousy time to stiffen. I have always been afraid of guns, but there is something about seeing a man wearing a pistol that excites me. I've never even touched a kid's air rifle or acted on an impulse to seduce a man who hunted, but there I was, horny as hell, with no prospects for even a lousy blind date. Adding to my misery, my randy body put me in the awkward position of needing to brush the kitten in the worst way while stuck in a very public place—over half a day before Sydney could take the edge off.

Now at the podium, the bailiff called out names of the people selected for the jury to try a woman accused of murdering her husband. My heart raced when he said, "Mary," but my stomach curdled when "Ann Bernadetto" followed. No more Marys were called. Shut out again. *Shit*.

I glared at my watch to see how long it was to lunch time and relief. When I looked up, I noticed a not bad looking man, young enough to consider dragging into a restroom stall, looking at me from the other side of the room. His creamlike complexion contrasted with his dark, almost black hair—most likely Irish. I strolled to the multi-stall ladies only to pee and primp. Not wanting to be too obvious, I waited until my return trip to get a closer look.

He was taller than me and had large hands. I thought they might rival Sydney.

I stopped in my tracks when the bailiff thumped the microphone. "Listen up," he boomed. "You're excused for lunch now, but be back by one."

I wondered what to do without being too obvious. I stretched my spine to full height, pulled my shoulders back and took tiny steps while not looking in his direction.

"Excuse me, miss. I'm a stranger here and don't

know where to eat," rolled out of his mouth, into my left ear. "Do you know where a guy could get a grinder and a frappe?"

"You're not from Jersey, are you?" I asked with my best come-hither look, recognizing his Boston accent. He spoke in complete sentences. He'd surely be good enough for one night.

"There's no hiding that," he said with a sly smile.

"I don't know my way around here either." I had had no need of the courthouse since Isaac didn't file charges and I hadn't needed a marriage license yet.

"Maybe we could search for something together."

"Okay." He wasn't toned like an athlete but wasn't flabby. Our daughter would be tall.

"Better get moving if we're going to get back on time." He swung his hand chivalrously to let me lead the way, and I swayed my happy hips out of the courthouse.

On the way to Blue Moon Café, Ken and I introduced ourselves and shared our backgrounds, the G-rated version in my case. He was attractive and pleasant company, although not particularly witty nor well read. Our lunch conversation found its way to current movies with no prompting from me.

"*The Boys from Company C* is out now," he said. "It's getting good reviews."

Vietnam on a first date? Too intense. "How about *California Suite?* Maggie Smith is always great."

Neither of us was assigned to a jury that afternoon, allowing us to be released early. This reprieve gave Ken time to do to me what Maggie Smith's character wanted

Michael Caine to do to her before we caught the early show. He was considerably less experienced and imaginative than many of my lovers, but he applied himself enthusiastically. Having brought a change of clothing and toiletries, in case I had been sequestered, shielded me from doing the slut walk in front of the jury pool the next morning.

๛

Although I had had far more intellectual discussions with three-year-olds, Ken and I dated happily for several months. We spent our weekends going to movies, hiking, eating casual dinners, though nothing resembling Tom Jones style. He didn't exactly chimi my changa, but our sex was more than adequate.

My now audible clock triggered a change in my attitude about intercourse. I no longer wanted a sperm donor, turkey baster or otherwise, starting my daughter. She was going to have a father, and a real one like I had. Spreading my legs switched from being a chore necessary to attract and keep a boyfriend to dress rehearsal practice for my daughter's conception. When I was bored or Ken was taking too long, I imagined what it would be like to play with my little girl in the park near the yellow clapboard house where we would live. He was amiable, not demanding intercourse all the time, and let me blow him as often as I liked. We rarely argued.

When Ken's company transferred him back to Boston to work on a new project, he forced me to make a decision. I had to decide whether I would go with him or stay where I was. This was my most normal relationship since my first one, and I wanted it to continue. But I liked my job, and North Jersey had become only the second place I'd call home. I learned to drive here and knew all the streets by name. Every six months, my hairdresser cut my hair just the same way, and the dentist was so gentle I got all the recommended check-ups for the first time in my life. Most of all, the corner pet store always had the cutest puppies in its window.

Having no office romances to dilute my efforts, I performed even better than usual and looked forward to a promotion. The pay increase would enable me to buy a more reliable car with affordable payments. I'd always been terrified my cars would crap out, leaving me stranded in rush hour traffic on the Turnpike. I might even have enough money left over to take a cruise. Love or money? Such a choice. Being poor so long on the one hand and never having had a successful relationship, on the other, put me in a quandary. I vacillated back and forth until little time remained to make a decision.

The afternoon of the day before Ken's departure, while returning from a meeting on another floor, I heard someone say my name and others chuckle. The tall cubicle walls hid the talkers from view. I stopped to eavesdrop unseen on their gossiping about me.

"Oh no, Jim will get that promotion," said a female voice I thought I recognized.

"I don't follow," said a male I hadn't heard before.

"If a regulator turns down one of our drugs for marginal reasons," said a man with authority, "and it's one she really wants approved—"

A catty woman with a nasal voice interrupted, "Well, let's just say his wouldn't be the first desk she crawled under to get her way."

"He may be the only man in North Jersey she hasn't piped," said the second male voice.

They all laughed. Shame and embarrassment engulfed me. I raced to the restroom so no one would see me crying. *Why do they have to be so nasty? Everybody else dates around until they find someone. And all the guys here have asked me out. They had some interest in me. I don't understand. What did I do wrong?*

After gathering myself in the ladies' room, I returned to my desk and called Ken.

"I'm coming with you," I said, trying to sound cheerful.

"You'll really like Boston. It's wicked great. Let's celebrate." Ken sounded ecstatic in his now heavier accent.

"I'll be busy tonight packing. A million things to do." I looked forward to moving but viewed it more as an escape than embarking on a new adventure.

I spent much of the afternoon writing a résumé for the first time, having worked at Carver-Watkins since high school. That finished, I wrote a simple letter of resignation and stuffed my few personal items in a cardboard box. I killed time disinfecting my cubicle like I did every week until my boss's light turned off. *One thousand one, one thousand two…one thousand ten.*

I placed my resignation on the exact center of her blotter and set my badge and office key on top of it.

On the way home, I picked up Boston newspapers. That night, I sent out a few cover letters and résumés. Too little time remained to conduct a job search before we left, but I landed a decent position shortly after we settled into a comfortable apartment.

I liked life in Boston, including working in a boy's dorm where the terminal to the computer on which the company bought time was located—very cool—but the students were much too young for a mature woman such as myself, even for dalliances.

My work involved analyzing glaucoma data, which was very interesting and had the added benefit of acquainting me with the MTA. I always made sure I had plenty of change and small bills on me in case they raised the fare like they did in the song about poor old Charlie.

Every day I followed the same schedule. I printed out reports run overnight on the terminal. In my dorm room-turned office, I analyzed the reports, checked for data errors and made corrections to those files and prepared new ones for ongoing analyses. After lunch, I took the MTA to the university computing center to submit my new runs. I walked from there to the company office for new instructions, should there be any.

I loved my job and its routine. I could count on it. Then, I went home and took advantage of what Boston had to offer sophisticated college-educated women in their late twenties.

Things were the best they'd ever been in my adult

life until I tired of Ken. Living with him revealed that he wasn't as smart as I had previously thought. I needed more stimulation, and he had no interest in intellectual pursuits. Maybe my love for him wore off. Who knows? I had hoped things would be different this time, but they weren't. It's good I made sure I didn't get pregnant. My daughter was going to have her father's name and wouldn't come from a broken home.

I started wondering if my unhappiness with Ken was affecting my well-being. I was normally very healthy, but I'd started feeling poorly in the mornings. My stomach was upset, I couldn't keep breakfast down, I felt bloated, and my period was late. That was the strangest part because I'm very regular. The only time I had been irregular before was in hopeful anticipation of Tim devirginizing me when I visited him at the air base. But he didn't, and I got regular again, real quick. It might've been emotional. Or I might have been—

Son of a bitch. I can't be—

Sometimes denial was so much more convenient.

Ken nagged me to see a doctor. The nurse took blood, urine, and saliva samples. The doctor probed me in what had to be all of my orifices. Instead of going home to wait for the results, I sat in the waiting room for an hour reading a mystery novel. *Trying* to read was more accurate. I started the same chapter at least six times, but couldn't recall having read any of it before. Unable to concentrate, I set the book aside and fidgeted. I tried unsuccessfully to put cancer out of my mind. Granny was fighting breast cancer, but she smoked. It can be hereditary, but Mom was healthy, and she was a whole lot older than me. My sister Beth was fine, too.

The nurse eventually called my name. I started to follow her back to the examination room but suddenly needed to pee in the worst way. After making a short stop, I waited patiently in the little room for the results. In a few minutes, the doctor walked in with a big grin on her face.

"Hi, Mom."

"I think you've got the wrong chart."

"Mary Louise?"

I nodded. The butterflies in my stomach metamorphized into bumblebees.

"You'll both be just fine. You're healthy and have good bone structure. You'll have no trouble carrying him or her."

"You've got to be kidding. I have an IUD."

"Nothing's a hundred percent."

Fuck me! This can't be happening. I did everything right. I had all the prescribed inspections after the IUD was inserted. I religiously checked the string to make sure it was still in place. They must have made a mistake. Whenever I suspected in the least that something might be wrong, I had it checked immediately. I couldn't be pregnant. Sure, I knew no birth control was one hundred percent, but I didn't mess mine up like stupid girls do. It just wasn't fair. *Shit. Piss. Fuck. Cunt!*

I had to do something about it ASAP. A few years earlier, I'd offered Tim to carry his baby and parent her by myself—only if it was a girl—and give it to him if it was a boy. Now that I had an actual bun in the oven, it was an entirely different matter. To begin with, I made him an offer he'd refused, and I knew I wouldn't have to make good on it. Secondly, I would've liked to have had his baby. He treated me well, and our children would've been very smart. I just didn't want to marry him. Looking back, I knew I would've been happier with Tim if he'd stood up to me and didn't let me lead him around by the nose. No way was I going to carry Ken's child. No way was I going to end up trapped in a marriage like Mom.

Damn. I didn't want a baby—yet. I didn't want to end up like my mother.

I walked half a block to my bank's nearest branch and drew out a thousand to cover upcoming expenses, then drove to Planned Parenthood and scheduled an abortion for two days later. I picked up New York and Jersey newspapers on the way to Ken's apartment.

"How'd it go?" He seemed sincere.

"Lab results won't be back for a few days. Can't have sex until then."

He looked downcast. "It's been awhile."

He picked up his bowling bag, kissed me goodbye, and walked out the door oblivious to what was happening.

"Good luck tonight."

He would have married me, but I didn't want to marry him. I called friends and former co-workers to get information on the North Jersey job market and asked if they'd get me some leads.

I found a few possibilities in the New York papers,

typed up cover letters, and fired off some résumés.

Just as I was leaving for the post office, Sybil, a friend who had mentored me in the rituals of bar-banging when I was just starting to get naked with men, called back. She told me a friend of hers knew of an opening her management was desperate to fill and that I should get a résumé in the mail and call them in the morning. I did. The boss wanted to interview me the following day, but I put him off until the end of the week.

After hanging up with what I hoped would soon be my next employer, I told my Boston boss I was quitting immediately due to a family emergency, then I bought a large bottle of Advil and a big box of Kotex, filled up my MGB with gas, and headed for the apartment. I'd almost finished packing my car when Ken arrived home from work.

He spotted my suitcases and looked dazed. "Tooks, what're you doing?"

"Things just haven't worked out between us. It's not you, it's me." I couldn't help having a preference for guys with brains.

He placed himself between me and the door. "Where're you going?"

"Don't know yet. Somewhere in Jersey. I'll write when I have an address." I pecked his cheek goodbye, pushed past him, trotted out to my car, and threw my suitcases into it.

Ken followed me out. "Tookie, what's wrong?"

"There were things I thought I wanted, but just not right now."

He looked pathetic, broken that I was leaving with no warning. "I can change."

"I've crawled under my last desk," I shouted and drove away.

ഇ

I spent the night in an inexpensive motel near the clinic.

Ever hear of an IUD baby? I'm a statistician, so I'll use numbers to explain what happened. Let's say the IUD is ninety-nine percent effective in preventing a pregnancy. Ninety-nine percent's a pretty high number, so let's put it to the test. Assume a woman has penetrative intercourse once every third day—much less often than I did back then—and her IUD had been installed properly.

Fortunately—or not, depending on one's perspective—a woman can only get pregnant four or five days a month: when she's ovulating. Five days out of twenty-eight sounds like a low risk, but pesky sperms sometimes hang around for a few days longer, extending the danger zone. My tendency to be especially horny while ovulating probably doubled or tripled my risk. Ninety-nine percent effective also means one percent ineffective, and you're preggers, even if your device works properly. My number must've been long overdue. Probabilities were against me. If I hadn't been so careful with my birth control, I would've been knocked up and had abortions years earlier. I wanted the next time to be the right time.

I gave a fictitious name and paid the clinic in cash.

The procedure went smoothly with no significant after effects. No way was I making a record of this by turning it in to my insurance company. I slapped a Kotex into place, hopped into my car, and hit the road with far too much on my mind to feel anything, either positive or negative, about the abortion. I focused on driving to my old haunts. During a rest stop, I called a motel near the interview site to make a reservation. I'd be arriving later than I liked and needed to get as much rest as possible before my mid-morning appointment.

I carried my bags into the room and dropped them on the floor before collapsing on the bed, crying uncontrollably. Soon, the pillow was soaked with my tears. I tossed it aside to use another of the several that covered half of the double bed. I cried until I felt twenty pounds lighter.

I felt…relief—I was no longer pregnant—and fell into a deep sleep. I dreamt I was pushing a little girl who looked like me, except for having fewer freckles, on a swing. Both of us giggled. In another scene, I sat in the driveway adjusting the roller skates on the same girl when she was six, just like I had done for my little brothers and the neighborhood kids when I was a teenager. In a scene that recalled painful memories, Mother stumbled around the house dragging a huge beer bottle and slurring her words while I, crying, searched desperately for a way to make her happy.

The next morning, I stuffed the Advil and as many Kotex as I could into my purse as a precaution. The interview went fine. I wasn't super, and definitely not a perfect fit for the job, but they were in a bind and needed someone pronto. I was just the girl to get the job done right.

My new company competed with Carver-Watkins but was much larger. Former coworkers soon knew I was back in the area because a few had switched jobs in my absence and were working for the new company. So, I necessarily cleaned up my act at work, which meant no more getting laid while getting paid—either in the office or with coworkers outside of work. I wanted to move up the food chain and wasn't about to do anything to thwart my chances.

It was 1979, and I'd been in this locale twelve years, except for my stint in Boston. That was almost a decade longer than anywhere else I'd lived before. I felt comfortable here and determined to stay forever.

The work at the new company was far more interesting than I expected. I analyzed suture data for a major supplier of various products used to close wounds and incisions. Their computing facilities were far better than my last job.

Looking around the office, it soon became clear that graduate degrees were necessary for advancement. Without one, I wouldn't move up. My alma mater offered a master's degree in applied statistics that emphasized pharmaceutical studies.

My new employer provided education reimbursement, and New Jersey State's graduate programs were offered nights and weekends. This was perfect for me. Attending grad school would give me opportunities to meet new guys. More intelligent ones with more intelligent genes.

CHAPTER 3

Leaf-Peeping with Larry

I stopped going to mass when I started living on my own because the Catholic Church heaps too much guilt on you. Forget about confession. I won't do that anymore. I didn't mind church as a kid. In fact, I have some good memories, such as my First Communion. Dad said, "You're so beautiful, you could go right up to heaven and be an angel," when he saw me in my white dress that looked like a bridal gown. But no way was I going to tell some priest about my love life.

Neighbors and friends at work told me good things about a liberal church near my apartment. The minister preached uplifting sermons and spewed almost no fire and brimstone. "Merry Methodist" as locals called the church, attracted middle class, college-educated WASPs, including several single males, to the eleven o'clock service. Both the congregation and the liturgy differed greatly from the working-class Catholic churches I attended as a child. As soon as mass ended, Catholics dashed out of the church for home or to a tavern, where the Merry Methodists hung around for coffee, doughnuts, and the many activities, committees, and interest groups the church sponsored. They were essentially Unitarians without the bumper stickers.

My parents' Catholic friends talked about the hardships strikes created for their families. My Merry Methodist friends discussed vacations, investments, hobbies, causes, and the latest Broadway shows. The Catholics' music may have been more beautiful having been written by great composers and sung by trained choirs. But the Protestant hymns were more upbeat and fun to sing, provided you flipped to the proper page in the hymnal quickly enough.

I liked the bell choir best. Not having any musical background, the bell choir gave me the opportunity to make music with little training. I enjoyed ringing the hand bells, but never really mastered the technique for ringing two of them at the same time. They were just too heavy for me to hold and control with one hand. Our director was kind of dorky, but fun to be around. He tried to appear serious, but did goofy things like having us play the first few bars of the wrong song, then act shocked when *Twinkle, Twinkle Little Star* came out instead of *Silent Night.*

I dressed to attract whenever we performed because we were seated up front in full view of the entire congregation. I got hit on a lot. That was the upside. The downside was that most of the guys who treated me to lunch afterward were religious.

The first Sunday after Labor Day, during our first concert of the fall, I caught a guy eyeballing me. The wide fan-shaped interior gave churchgoers a clear view of the minister, choir, and anyone else at the front of the church. The seating area sloped downward toward the pulpit sort of like in an old movie theater, giving me a clear view of the congregation. The first time he looked at me, I did nothing. The second time, I smiled. The third time, I winked. He stopped staring and turned his head. I kept a straight face—barely. Great fun. I couldn't tell much about him from a distance other than he looked like an accountant.

The service finished, I turned to put my hand bells away. But, before I could take a step, I felt someone else's heel tramp down on my arch, causing me to drop my bells.

"Ow!" *Better milk this for all it's worth.*

He blushed, as if embarrassed for his clumsiness. "I'm sorry."

"This how you meet women?" I grabbed his upper arm for balance then sat on a nearby folding chair and rubbed my supposedly aching foot.

"What can I do? I can get some ice from the kitch-en."

He was a little taller than me, skinny, with light brown hair, reddish cheeks with a few pock marks, rather ordinary looking overall, not handsome, not ugly, but his being interested in meeting me improved his prospects.

Let's see what he drives. "Can you call me a cab?"

"Driving you home is the least I can do." I hung onto

his arm while I hobbled slowly in the early autumn shade along the oak-lined path to the parking lot and his car.

The morning after my birthday celebration, I'd widened my selection criteria to include many men I'd previously ignored. I didn't want to miss Mr. Right just because he hid his full potential. I figured I'd have to kiss some frogs before I found my prince, so I didn't let a few hundred lousy kisses deter me. I kissed a lot of things to get what I wanted.

He opened the door of his low-slung, fire engine red Porsche convertible for me. I knew getting into it wearing a dress could be a challenge. Yes, I broke down and bought two church dresses, both green, both modest, but stylish, picked because they displayed my attributes in their best light. I hated wearing dresses, but I attracted more men when I did. Lots more. Bummer.

"Watch your head. It's low."

"No problem. My first boyfriend had a Classic T-Bird." I backed up to the seat, sat down, and swung my legs in, showing him a little thigh. His eyes followed my every movement, at least from my ass to my knees.

"Lunch? How 'bout the new place across town people at work are raving about?"

Never heard of the place, but this guy seems safe. "Fine. Where's work?" I liked the feel of the leather seats on my bottom and the new car smell.

"At the air base."

"So, you're a fighter pilot?" *No way is he a jet jockey.*

"No, I'm an accountant."

"In what kind of plane?" Acting stupid threw shy guys.

Somewhat flustered, he sputtered, "On the ground in the procurement office. I keep track of the cost of repair parts."

I figured as much. But he could surely support a family. The Porsche would have to go when the baby arrived. He looked like he was pushing forty and his body didn't do much for me, but he was agreeable company.

"Aren't you seeing whatshername?" I asked when he tried to kiss me at the door to my apartment. I'd seen him with that skinny mouse who sings alto in the choir.

"We decided to see other people."

"I don't feel like throwing you on my bed and having my way with you, Larry, but I'd like to see you again."

"S-Saturday?" He stuttered or blushed every time I unexpectedly said something remotely sexual. He looked cute.

"Pick me up at six."

⌦⌫⌦

Although he wasn't the most stimulating conversationalist I dated, Larry kept up on current events and, for a bonus, he sustained conversations better than I could. He treated me like a lady and didn't pressure me for sex. Instead, he deferred to me. He had far less experience. Larry was the first guy, since Tim, who didn't expect me to put out after he spent a couple of bucks on me.

I wasn't in love with him or even infatuated, but I'd

had much worse companions. Larry was always kind and considerate, and he tried hard to please me in and out of bed. After several dinner and movie dates, I arranged to spend a weekend leaf-peeping in Vermont.

"Tookie," he said, upon opening the door to an over-priced, uninspiring room at the back of a single-floor 1950s economy motel, "I wanted to take you to a nicer place than this."

"I wanted that, too, but all the better places are full up. Leaf peepers book rooms a year in advance. I was lucky to find a cancellation." I flung open the drapes on the picture window. "What a view!" It took my breath away. I'd never seen such vivid colors before—bright yellows, oranges, reds, dark reds, with some greens and browns thrown in.

"We can take it in from the Adirondack chairs as soon as we unpack." Larry was already placing his socks and underwear neatly in the dresser.

"Let's go for a walk. Unpack later." I grabbed my room key and headed out the door.

He trotted after me. "Okay. A short one."

"I want to get the most out of this glorious fall day. We won't have many more like it, and this one's mostly over."

"The sugar maples *are* the most vivid I've ever seen."

"Enjoy them with me."

He reached out for me. I enjoyed walking hand in hand down the path from the parking lot into the solitude of the woods. Fall is my favorite season. I like feeling its warm sunshine against my skin and spending cool evenings by a fire. Smelling the dry fall air and breathing it in also sharpens my many appetites.

"My legs are tired," he whined after only a half hour. "Here's a path back."

"Whatever. I want to take this in as long as I can."

He trudged back along the wide, well-worn path alone. Soon, I was deep in my thoughts and took in the gorgeous surroundings as I sauntered along the trail.

I felt stale in bed. I hadn't developed a new technique in ages, and most of the ones I knew benefited the guy a whole lot more than me. I picked up a long stick to help me up a steep incline and threw it away at the top. That skinny stick reminded me of how little sex I was getting. I'd exhausted Larry's limited repertoire in our first two weekends and had nothing exciting to look forward to.

I skipped flat rocks across a small pond at the side of the trail to distract myself. The reflections of the trees on the water swayed when the ripples crossed them. I'd thought I was done studying techniques, but I was so bored, I needed a refresher course. One of the many good things about reading sex manuals is that I get horny. I almost came the night before just reading about the Rusty Trumpet. A good one would surely buckle my knees. I couldn't remember the last time a motel manager told me to quiet down because he was getting complaints. I missed that.

I picked a bouquet of the most colorful leaves to take home with me, thinking they'd brighten up my apartment.

The problem with the Rusty Trumpet is that I needed a man to give it to me. No guy would give me one without getting a Rusty Trombone first. That was the rub. That was one place I wasn't wild about putting my tongue. But I decided to Toss the Salad once to get a Rusty Trumpet. A great orgasm would definitely be worth a little inconvenience. It might even be like a lot of things that seem gross until you try them. The Rusty Trombone might be a good trick to have in my bag. Maybe that was why I hadn't found the right guy yet. I needed to give them more variety. I was so good at what I did, men would do most anything I asked—in bed. For a while. But most showed me no consideration out of bed. Maybe Larry could be talked into doing it.

I started to shiver because I'd lost track of time. The air temperature had plunged when the sun dropped low in the sky. Its rays still warmed, but the air cooled. Was I horny because the cold air made my nipples erect, or had thinking about orgasming done it?

Regardless, I was chilly and invigorated and wanted to try something new. A cool breeze pushed me forward as I trotted back to the room.

Larry was shy. Not very muscular, he never went without a shirt. He preferred having sex in the dark but would do it in the daylight with the drapes drawn and the room darkened whenever I asked.

I, on the other hand, loved to show off and urged my partners to watch me closely.

They needed to realize how much thought, skill, and effort I put into pleasuring them. Guys didn't applaud me like opera audiences cheer a diva, but they should have. They just soaked it in. Just saying I was great wasn't enough. It showed they didn't fully value my efforts. Maybe a stranger would happen by the window and appreciate how dedicated I was to my craft.

CHAPTER 4

Larry in the Shower

Passing a downed tree in a spot with a particularly spectacular view, I debated stopping. On the one hand, pun intended, this would have been a perfect place to serenade unseen strangers with my wails of pleasure while, let us say, playing a solo on my cello instead of waiting to play a duet in my room. Having to wait versus warmth and comfort? I'd played solos the entire week since I'd last been with Larry. That he brought with him the one thing no woman has, but what most of us enjoy spending quality time with, swung the balance in favor of returning to the motel. I raced the rest of the way back to the object of my affection.

When I burst into the room, ready for adventure, I found shy Larry had closed the drapes. In hopes a stranger might happen by and appreciate my performance, I yanked the cord and opened wide the drapes covering the picture window. Happenings in the room were now exposed to the outside world, almost like the windows in Amsterdam's red-light district. Hearing the shower running, I realized I had an opportunity to try something I'd recently studied but hadn't performed on a man yet.

I stripped down in record time, flinging my clothes to all corners of the room, before silently entering the spartan tiled room containing only a commode, tub with shower and minimal cheap chrome accessories. The sink and mirror were out in the bedroom. His eyes closed to keep soap out of them and his hearing diminished by the running water and noise from adjacent rooms, Larry shampooed his hair in the cast-iron tub that doubled as a shower, unaware of my presence.

I lathered my hands before spooning him, but he interrupted my plan by jumping a foot when my love brush caressed his buns.

"What the—" His overreaction showed I had successfully surprised him. Apparently sensing something wonderful was in store for him, he looked at me over his shoulder, his face covered with an uneasy grin.

"Calm down. You'll enjoy this." I reached around him and clutched his limp lizard with my soapy right hand and his jewels with the left. He froze. My hip gyrations rubbed my soft red bristles against his bum, waking my favorite delicacy. A few trombone strokes transformed Little Larry's balsa into oak.

As a sensitivity test and to make sure he was clean enough for what I had in mind, I slid my well soaped middle finger up his crack. He flinched, of course, but not as much as expected.

He was ready for something he'd never forget.

"Rinse off now." I rotated him around in the heaviest spray of water until his back was to the nozzle. I made sure all the soap was off his vital areas before turning off the water. I handed him a towel, saying, "Dry off. Start with your hair."

I pressed myself against him, front to front, then slowly slid downward, kissing his body along the way, ending on my knees in front of him. When my lips aligned perfectly, I gave him a little suck. "Hold still."

"What's that ringing?" His voice had an odd tone.

"Shssh. Forget the damn phone. I don't hear it. Let's have fun."

"My head. It feels funny," he grunted then stumbled backward against the wall.

His feet pushed against my legs, causing me to fall away from him, bumping my head against the sloping end of the tub before landing on my back, soaking my hair.

Larry's legs buckled. He gripped the shower curtain tightly but down it came, rod and all into the tub, as his legs flew out from under him, landing on top of me. His body twisted as he fell, entangling him in the cheap plastic adorned with maple leaves and New England scenes. *Bam.* Larry's face hit the tub's water spout. *Thuck.* His head slammed against the top of the cast-iron tub like a ripe melon.

His dead weight pinned me down. Struggling didn't get me out from under him. Pushing against him accomplished nothing except tiring me.

"Get up!"

No response.

I finally pulled one my legs out from under him and then, with a lot of exertion, the other. But he didn't move. "Larry, Larry!"

Still no response.

I pulled the rest of myself out from under him and, with much slipping and sliding, got to my feet. Looking down from a standing position, I couldn't tell much. Running cold water on Larry's face didn't revive him. He was dead to the world, if not actually dead, and bleeding profusely.

I climbed out of the tub to run to call for help, but my feet flew out from under me on the slick, wet linoleum floor. I landed hard, flat on my can. Rolling over onto all fours, I crabcrawled to the phone next to the bed and dialed nine-one-one.

"Help! Come quick! He might be dying!" I tried unsuccessfully not to panic.

"Calm down and tell me what happened," asked a disembodied female voice in a heavy New England accent.

"My boyfriend is lying in the bathtub, bleeding, and unconscious."

"What is your location?" asked the flat voice.

"In a dumpy motel in Vermont."

"Which motel?"

"Uh…uh…Shady Glen, Rusty Shade, uh, uh." *I might have to stumble outside bare-assed naked to look at the sign.*

"Shady Rest?"

"That's it." *Phew.* "You oughta be able to find this place. It's on a kinda main road."

With a tone that sounded less than pleased with me, she responded, "We know where it is. Which room?"

"Uh…uh…shit!" I didn't know that either.

"Look at your room key." She sounded condescending.

I didn't remember where I put mine. Had I left it in the door? Better check. Just then, I looked down and saw Larry's lying on the table next to the phone. "Here it is. One-thirteen."

"Is he breathing?"

"I think so."

She exhaled loudly. "Please check."

Afraid of falling again on the slick, wet floor, I crabcrawled back to the bathroom and shook Larry. He seemed to be alive but didn't wake up. I crawled back to the phone. "He's breathing but still unconscious."

"Cover him with a blanket to keep him warm. Motels often have spares in the closet."

"Okay." Taking no chances, I crawled to the closet, where I pulled myself up by the doorknobs and steadied myself by holding onto the door. Nothing. Not even on the shelf above the clothes bar. I crawled back to the bed, snatched its only blanket and took it to the bathroom. After unsuccessfully trying to wake him again, I spread the blanket over Larry, then crawled back to the phone.

"He's still out, but I covered him with a blanket."

"Help's on the way. Keep calm." That was easy for

her to say. When you think you've killed a man, you panic.

A siren shrieked so loudly, it could have been in the parking lot. I looked out the window. It wasn't there yet, but it was getting louder by the second. Just then, I real-ized I was butt naked, and my hands and arms were cov-ered with Larry's blood from trying to revive him. I couldn't tell them what I did. I might have killed him.

I crawled as quickly as I could back to the shower and tossed the blanket out of the way. Forcing my foot between Larry and the tub to straddle him, I rinsed the blood off me. Reviving him still didn't work, so I got out of the tub and covered him again.

A second siren came from another direction. Then another.

My feet turned cold from water dripping onto them. I needed to dry off. I couldn't do anything about Larry but didn't need to. Wasn't one normally naked when shower-ing? There was no time to dress him anyway. I had to look out for myself.

I frantically flipped through the clothes hanging in the closet next to the bathroom hoping to find a bathrobe. I only found an ironing board, some wire hangers, and Larry's clothes.

Bam, Bam, Bam—Bam, Bam, Bam. An impatient knock rattled the door. Bright lights shined through the picture window illuminating dripping-wet, naked me. "Let us in."

"Gimme a second," I shouted as I ducked into the bathroom to grab a towel. It took me a few seconds to wrap it around me and adjust it to not quite cover both essential areas at the same time.

The emergency vehicles, cars, and pickups pulling in made quite a racket. Firemen and EMTs bustled past the picture window.

Bam, Bam, Bam. "We need to get in. Now!"

I raced to the door, turned the knob, and jerked it open.

"Where is he?" The fortyish EMT looked at me and did a double take before asking again, "Where is he?" His pimply-faced teenaged trainee gawked at me.

I pointed to the bathroom. "In there."

Volunteer firemen came in pushing the EMTs farther into the room.

A gaggle of emergency personnel, leaf peepers, and curious locals gaped through the window and open door, snickering. A rent-a-cop tried to push the civilian onlookers back. I then realized that if I could see their faces, they could see me.

"I'm from *The Courier.* Who's in charge here?" asked a youngish male voice.

Damn. This fiasco must have been the most entertainment this burg ever got.

"You have to wait," said the cop.

I was nearly exposed to half the county, mostly wet, with EMTs and firemen ogling me instead of tending to Larry. This was not the type of attention even a wannabe exhibitionist desired. I freaked out, flinging the towel wide open, screaming, "Is this want you wanna see?" I turned to the voyeurs at the window. "How about you?"

The window gapers looked astonished but didn't leave or deflect their eyes from the sideshow.

I closed the towel and turned back to the EMTs. "Now get the hell in the bathroom and take care of Larry."

The EMTs ducked their heads sheepishly and trotted into Larry while the firemen rushed out the door.

Regaining my composure and forgetting I'd just shown them everything I had, I scanned the room, looking frantically for my clothes. Finding my slacks in one corner, I jerked them up over my wet, cold, naked bottom and under the towel, exposing it only briefly to the gawkers looking in the window. I recalled seeing the blue oxford shirt Larry wore driving up hanging in the closet. It would have to do, even if it made me look flat. Not wanting to expose what I didn't have again, I faced into the closet and put on his shirt, leaving the tail hanging out. I let the towel drop to the floor before buttoning the front.

Even though rough seams irritate my sensitive parts, I freebuffed in this emergency. *Ouch!* My butt hurt when I plopped down in a chair to put on my socks. No way would I let these yokel EMTs touch me, especially there.

While searching for my loafers, I saw myself in the mirror. I looked like shit. My hair would have scared Medusa. With no time to dry and comb it, I wrapped it in a towel like in a headscarf, a la Lucy Ricardo. Just then, an empty stretcher rolled into the room past me.

"Is he all right? What're you doing with him? Where're you taking him?"

The lead EMT stopped. A quizzical look formed on

his face when he looked at me. "We're taking him to the hospital. You can ride with us or go in your car."

"How do I get to the hospital?"

"Follow us."

A couple of minutes later, they wheeled Larry past me. He was awake, sort of, but incoherent.

At least I hadn't killed him.

As they loaded him into the ambulance, I gathered his wallet, car keys, room key, and glasses from the night stand. Larry was OCD, just like me—except when I'm in heat. I slipped on my loafers, zipped out of the room, and slammed the door behind me. Pushing my way through the nosey creeps still hanging around, I hopped into Larry's sports car, easing my banged-up bottom gently down onto the driver's seat.

A cub reporter, who probably thought this was a big story, knocked on my window. I ignored him, started the Porsche, and followed the ambulance out of the parking lot onto County Road 196.

I didn't know where we were going or how far it was. I knew we headed west because the rays of the setting sun blinded me until I closed the gap with the ambulance. Fearful I'd get lost if I stopped at a light, I kept on its tail as it raced through the few red lights we encountered. Keeping so close also limited my visibility. Ten excruciating minutes of almost blind driving seemed like an hour.

We arrived at a nondescript red-brick community hospital that looked like it'd been expanded each of the last several decades, each time in a different style. I angled Larry's car into the nearest parking space, probably a doctor's, and raced into the reception area, arriving there before the EMTs had unloaded him.

Checking Larry in went easy because, fortunately, his Blue Cross/Blue Shield policy covered out-of-state accidents. I gave the receptionist the phony name I used back then, before hotels required credit cards, and forged a fictitious signature on the admittance form. I didn't want my real name showing up in any records, knowing all-too-well how small-town newspapers cover fire, police, and ambulance calls. We women hated seeing our names in crime reports, not as much because we didn't want people knowing what we did, but for the personal information newspapers revealed, starting with your age. I could write it for them:

EMTs found tourist Lawrence Sorensen, 37, unconscious and bleeding in a bathtub at Shady Rest motel on County Road 196 yesterday afternoon. Whether Sorensen was a victim of a physical assault or a sex act gone awry isn't clear. When EMTs arrived, a woman, Mona Lotte, 25, was also in the room, naked and wet, as was the victim. Miss Lotte's part in the incident is still being determined...

Spying an empty seat in the darkest corner of the waiting room, I curled up to hide from prying eyes as much as one could in a molded plastic chair. Not surprisingly, others waiting to be treated or waiting for someone else gave me some odd looks. Country emergency rooms were essentially the same as their big city cousins, but smaller. Just subtract the armed guards and substitute bib overalls and flannel shirts for gang colors and Walmart women for hookers.

I love my long hair, and not just for how I use it to drive men wild. It's part of what makes me special. But it was wet, miles away from a hair dryer, being a royal pain in the ass. To say I was uncomfortable would be like calling a gallstone a minor irritation. Cold, wet water leaked out from under the towel, trickled down the back and sides of my neck, and formed icy rivers down my front and back on its way to where my panties should have been. Larry's thin cotton shirt was even less warm when wet.

I reached into my purse for a mirror but found the head scarf Larry had loaned me for the top-down drive up. Eureka! I hotfooted it to the ladies' room where I bent over under the hand dryer, rising only to spread different clumps of hair under the heat nozzle and to repound the start button a million times. I wasn't quite dry when the PA system bellowed:

"Lotte, Ms. Mona Lotte. Come to the receptionist's desk."

I twirled my mostly dry ratted hair into a large bun, hid as much of it as I could under the scarf, put on my sunglasses, and slinked to the receptionist's desk to answer her page. Seeing me appearing so differently, much of the room shot me skeptical looks accompanied by smirks and giggles. The receptionist handed me off to a volunteer who escorted me into the treatment room.

Larry lay bandaged and groggy on a gurney. The lump on his forehead had turned black and blue.

"You look awful," I said without thinking.

He didn't respond.

The ER doctor approached me. "We need your help. Mr. Sorensen is unable to tell us anything, and the EMTs weren't there when it happened. Fill us in, starting with his medical history."

"I don't know what he's had. We haven't been dating that long."

"Did he mention any allergies?"

Other than to a naked woman in the shower with him? "No, but I've seen him eat eggs and peanuts."

He marked a box on the form. "Can you describe exactly what happened right before he fell?"

"I wasn't there. I was out walking."

He looked skeptical. "Then tell us what you did see."

"When I came back to the room, I heard the shower running, so I read for a while. After five minutes or so, I knocked on the door to tell him to save some hot water for me. He hogs it, you know. He didn't answer. So, I went in and found him lying there with blood all over the place. He looked like he was dead, so I called nine-one-one."

"Did you try to revive him?"

"I ran some water over his head a couple of times, but it didn't work. I even slapped him. No response."

The doc looked me up and down suspiciously. "Had you been fighting?"

"No. He just got tired and came back to the room."

"How'd you get so wet and disheveled?"

Oh crap! He thinks I did it. "I didn't hit him."

"He's got a nasty gash on his face and a big lump on his head. Somebody or something did. Nurse, could you have the police send someone over?"

I had to come clean. "No need for that. I left something out."

"We thought you might have," the doc said with a sardonic smile while he poised his pen to take down notes.

"When I heard him showering, I got into the tub with him."

"Go on."

"He got aroused seeing me naked and passed out. That's all."

"That's probably not all, but it's enough. I can fill in the blanks." He looked as if he was disgusted with me.

"But, but—"

He turned away and signaled a nurse to come over to him. I eavesdropped on them as they walked away.

"I wouldn't be surprised if it was vasovagal syncope," he said to the nurse. "We get one or two of these every year, usually older men with their mistresses. We just need to treat his visible symptoms and keep him warm, so he doesn't go into shock. Better keep him here overnight for observation."

Vasovagal syncope? I'd never heard of that one before. What could it be?

Back in the waiting room, I got some cash from an out-of-network cash machine. No way was I going to pay for anything with my credit card. I didn't want these hayseeds to know my name. What I had intended to be a fun new experience for both of us had turned into utter humiliation.

Eventually, a nurse told me Larry should be okay after a night's rest. She gave him a sedative to ensure he'd sleep soundly and told me to come back in the morning.

⁊෨⁊෨

Famished by this time, but in no state to be seen in public, I returned to the Shady Rest. The owner wouldn't give me a different room. One wasn't available, it being peak leaf-peeping season and all. While I was away, the owner made a half-assed repair of the shower curtain and ran a vacuum cleaner over the carpet, part of it anyway. The room looked a lot worse than when we checked in, but it was a warm place to sleep, and nothing else was available within a hundred miles.

I showered and shampooed my hair, getting the jitters standing in the tub reflecting about what had happened to Larry. I didn't think I'd ever want to shower with a guy again. Definitely didn't want to make any more nine-one-one calls. Getting the tangles out was a nightmare. The fresh undies I put on after unsnarling it never felt so good.

I was starved but needed privacy. So, I headed to the nearest fast-food drive-thru. I'd avoided burger joints for years and feared the food would be inedible. I could've used a drink, but I never indulged. A sip of alcohol affected me so much I was afraid I'd lose control if I drank a whole glass of wine or can of beer.

I splurged with a Coke, a real Coke, not a diet one, a bacon cheeseburger, and fries. I constantly watched what I ate to keep my weight under control. Men wouldn't consider me at all if I let myself go. I had to look my best. But that night, I needed a pick-me-up, and I didn't want one of the male sort just yet. I opened up Larry's Porsche to get back to the motel before my meal congealed.

Instead of counting calories as I munched on the French fries, I pondered my future with Larry. With an entire evening on my hands with no place to go or anyone to spend it with, I fished my trusty sex manual out of the bottom of my suitcase. I always carried it on overnight trysts in case I got really lucky or incredibly bored. The index entry for fainting directed me to a section on *vaso-vagal syncope,* something I'd never heard of before that day. Men who had it passed out when blood rushed from their brains quickly. When I aroused Larry, his blood drained his brain to flood his penis, and he passed out. Having learned my lesson, the first time I blow a guy now, I have him stand next to a bed so he won't get hurt if he has VS. I wasn't about to give up the easiest way to keep a guy interested in me.

The hospital called early the next morning to tell me they'd be discharging Larry at ten. I gave the motel owner fifty dollars in cash—which he wouldn't report—to cover room damages. I left it up to him to contact Larry at his home if costs ran higher.

Larry smiled weakly at me from a wheelchair at the

receptionist's desk. He looked like hell with a large band-age over the cut on his check and the huge lump on his forehead. The doctor said he'd be fine, but he shouldn't drive for a few days. I didn't get much pleasure out of driving his Porsche the night before. But now that he was okay, and I didn't have to worry about jeopardizing our relationship, I had fun putting it through its paces on the back roads. With little traffic on Sunday morning, I got to feel his beast grip the pavement on tight turns at high speed.

"You're scaring me. Slow down."

Wimp. Some father you'd make. I'm dumping you to-day. I throttled back only a little because we'd be on the interstate all too soon. Smokies patrolled I-91 heavily in that season, so I behaved myself on the long, boring part of the trip home.

"Tooks, this isn't working."

Doing a mental happy dance for being let off the hook, I said, "Maybe you're right, Larry. You're probably better suited for whatshername in the choir."

"I suppose." He exhaled, shrinking down into his seat, looking resigned to his fate.

෧෨෧

I often saw Larry at church after that, generally at a distance, with neither of us making more than a polite greeting. Two weeks after our ill-fated trip, I saw him leave with the mouse. At Christmas, she flashed a rock on the third finger of her left hand so flagrantly, I'm sure she waved it for my benefit. Just after Memorial Day, I bumped into them going into the church.

"It's a beautiful day." I used my sweetest voice. Her butt was broader, and she had grown tits. He was fattening her up, or she was letting herself go after hooking him.

"Yes, it is."

If her looks could kill, I'd be dead a hundred times over. She had to know Larry and I'd been an item, even if only briefly.

"I need to get into my robe." She pulled him away by the arm.

A month later, I could no longer deny the truth. Worse yet, she looked cute in her maternity dress. I hated myself for being envious, but I could've been the one waiting for my daughter to arrive. Maybe I had been too hasty dropping Larry.

The first time they brought their baby to church, I avoided them but, thinking they'd head to the social room to show off their newborn after the service, I ran smack into them at the exit.

"Would you hold Mary Louise while I get something out of my purse, dear?" She looked pleased to be rubbing her good fortune in my face.

"Sure, hon." He took the baby from her and brought her closer to me.

"Nice name." I couldn't resist getting in that dig, but neither acknowledged it as such.

"We named her after our mothers, Mary and Louise."

How ironic was that? They gave their baby my name.

First, a guy who shot blanks, then a guy who didn't, and this time I missed getting my daughter when I threw back a wimp. The next guy would be better. He just had to be.

CHAPTER 5

Not on the First Date—for Once

The best thing that happened in 1979 was starting grad school at twenty-nine. The worst thing was my maternal grandmother, Gom, passing. Hers was the first loss of someone close to me. Gom and Pop were the only extended family I knew, and now Gom was gone. I would've loved to have lived near her growing up because she made me feel special.

My three younger brothers and older sister took up so much of Mom's time, she had little left for me. Gom's death created a large hole in my life that was only enlarged when Pop followed her less than a year later. Just thirty, I had no extended family left.

With Dad's health fragile, Mom drunk all the time, my only sister estranged and living distant from everyone, I felt alone in the world and wanted to start a family of my own.

❧❧❧

After standing in line for what seemed like an eternity in the gymnasium-turned-registration center to start my second semester of grad school, I finally reached the front. As enjoyable as my classes were, registration was still a drag. Taking two courses a semester, one on a weeknight and the other on the weekend would complete my master's degree in two years—provided I went summers and could get the classes I needed.

"Next," droned the plump young woman with no engagement ring, only a basic wedding band. She looked like might have been pregnant, but I couldn't tell for sure.

"Stats five-eighty-three and five-ninety." *Oh, please let there be seats this time.*

"They're both filled," she said, showing no concern for my plight.

My stomach churned. "But I need them. They're required prerequisites for everything else." *Only a slight exaggeration. Did I detect a tiny grin?*

"You can check with the department office. Perhaps they'll put you on a wait list. Next."

Through clenched jaws, I said, "Thanks." *For nothing.*

I stomped up the well-worn stairs in the 1960s institutional red-brick math building and stormed into the department office seeking assistance. I was shocked when I recognized that the scary reflection on the glass door was me. My advisor wasn't there, so I burst into the chair's office with nostrils flared. Lacking these courses, I'd never finish. Electives were available, but my program only allowed two.

The department chair must have recognized my distress, because he walked around his oversized administrator's desk and sat in an armchair facing me.

"Is there something I can do to help you?" he asked, looking into my eyes.

When I sputtered, slumped in the chair, unable to get anything out, he took my hand in his, patting it while waiting for me to calm enough to start. Staring at my hands, I unloaded on him. "This degree means a lot to me. I'm blocked from promotions at work without it." I rambled on and on about how I was alone in the world and had to support myself. He listened quietly, occasionally stroking my arm, until I finished, then simply asked, "What do you need most?"

My words spewed out. "Admit slips for five-eighty-three and five-ninety."

"Done." With that, he scribbled two special admission slips and handed them to me.

"It's that easy?" I couldn't believe this was all it took. I should have done this before.

He got up, walked behind me, where he gently caressed my tensed neck. "Yes."

"Why the hell did they put me through this crap if it's this damned easy?" My stomach calmed slightly. Had I known this was all it would take, I would have freaked out long ago.

He massaged my knotted shoulders while he talked. My tension eased, and I calmed down.

"We hold back a couple of seats to make sure the really serious students get in."

"Why do you think I'm serious?"

"I don't think it, I know it. You were the most studious one in my intro courses years ago."

"Really?" I was anxious to complete registration but thought better of bolting out the door before he finished saying whatever it was he wanted to say.

"Picture me with more hair."

"Oh, yeah. Professor Hay. I had to work hard in your classes."

"Please call me Milt, Tookie."

He babbled on about the quality of current undergrads and other topics of little concern to me. Nothing he said or did after giving me the admission slips registered. Euphoric, I left his office and literally skipped to the bookstore to get the required textbooks. I felt the best I had for a long time the two weeks before classes started, probably because I didn't worry about getting a late add slip this time.

A week after classes started, Professor Hay appeared out of nowhere and approached me as I walked down the hall. "Do you have a couple of minutes to discuss something, Tookie?"

"Can it keep? I'm meeting some classmates to plan our group project." I was in a hurry. Stats five eighty-three was an important course and the project counted for a third of the grade.

"Stop by my office when you can. Okay?"

"O—Okay." Administrative trivia. I didn't have time for nonsense.

⌘

Grad work was more difficult than undergrad, but I was better prepared. Working in the pharmaceutical industry over a decade gave me a huge leg up on my classmates. Getting better grades than the pretty girls had always boosted my ego.

Fronting tuition money was no longer a challenge. Finally making a living wage, I didn't need to practice the oldest profession to come up with tuition or to make ends meet. The downside was little free time for old boyfriends and hardly any to prowl for new ones. Maybe I'd meet a guy in one of my classes and treat myself to after-class trysts.

❧❧❧

I arrived at school ten minutes early before my next class to get the administrative BS out of the way. Prof. Hay sat behind the impressive walnut desk in front of his diploma-covered wall, fiddling with some papers. Hearing me enter, he looked up and smiled.

"Tookie, do you have a few minutes to chat now?" He seemed more serious than I had expected.

"I guess," I said with resignation. I wanted to get this over as quickly as possible so I could scout out guys in the Union.

"It's nice having students in the program who are as dedicated to the field as you are." His eyes locked onto me.

What's that tingling feeling? I looked down, hoping to be wrong, but my erect nipples poked at my T-shirt, pointing out what I didn't have. I didn't want them visible unless I was naked and always wore a bra in the winter when it was cold. I hid them from him by holding my notebook against my chest.

He was tall enough, strongly built, probably the most accomplished man I'd ever met. And he was powerful, something that always excited me in a man. He was a decade older than me and very polished. Milt finished his PhD a few months before I had even started my BA. He taught a few of my undergrad courses and called on me to answer questions occasionally, but nothing special.

Of course, I was quieter and much less sophisticated then. As all this rushed through my mind, he created a confusing situation. I twisted my hair, uncertain what he was up to.

"You're not the same freshman I met a decade ago. You've matured into a beautiful, sophisticated woman who I'd like to get to know better."

Wow! He put it right out there. I had always focused on studying and boys in his class, without noticing his interest in me.

"I wanted to get your opinion about some new courses we're considering adding to the curriculum." He looked at his watch before continuing. "We don't have much time before our classes start. We can talk more at dinner Friday at Chez Nous. Okay?"

He was the most confident man I'd ever been around, a major turn-on.

"Uh. Okay." Bewildered by the unexpected attention, I agreed without thinking.

He stood up, and I followed him. At the door, he said, "I'll pick you up at seven."

I just smiled and looked stupid. It was too late to call my more-experienced former co-worker to ask advice about dating a powerful older man when I got home that night, I'd have to wait until the next morning. Sydney prepared me for some most erotic dreams.

⋘⋙

Cynthia still worked at Carver-Watkins, and I called her just after her morning break.

"Congratulations," I said. "I hear you got married while I was away."

"Thanks. Still in Boston?" The former proper spinster sounded confused as to why I was calling.

"I'm back. Work at Jackson and Jackson now. Need advice about a man."

"You're asking me for advice?" She had been the one who gave me good advice I didn't follow when I was an eighteen-year-old virgin starting out at Carver-Watkins and sounded like she was trying to figure out why I was calling her.

"A guy your age asked me out, and I don't wanna botch this one."

"Don't sleep with him on the first date, if you want something serious."

"That much I figured out. I don't want to blow my chances for something long term."

"You want to marry him?" She sounded shocked after hearing—mostly true—salacious office gossip about me for years.

"Don't know yet. Might." He could give my daughter all the advantages I didn't have.

"Take things slowly. This may be a challenge for you, Tookie. Be a lady in all ways."

"Free for lunch? I want to hear everything about your wedding."

"Meet me at The Grille at one."

ↄჂↄჂ

Cynthia had been in the jungle longer than anyone, and I took her extensive advice to heart, by playing it cool and trying not to act overly interested all week. I didn't walk past Milt's office when on campus or peek when I heard his Oldsmobile pull up Friday night. My living room got its tenth once-over to make sure nothing was out of place. Per Cynthia's suggestion, I wore a conservative blouse with a high collar and remembered to maintain good posture, all to not look easy or needy.

Knock. Knock. The hands on the clock pointed exactly to twelve and seven.

My heart fluttered. *One thousand one, one thousand two, one thousand three.* I held myself back as long as I could and forced my legs not to run to greet him. After taking a deep breath to settle myself, I nonchalantly opened the door.

"Wine? For me?" Tim was the last one to give me anything but trouble. Milt was serious. "Thank you. Have a seat while I put this in the kitchen."

"But first." He pulled a white gardenia date out of his lapel and slipped it into my hair. It matched the expensive wool slacks I'd bought to contrast the emerald green silk blouse I took off layaway just for this date. Milt had me. He could've taken me right there on the coffee table with no resistance whatsoever. Not wanting him to see me blushing at my thoughts, I stepped into the kitchen, out of view. After fanning myself with the local muckraker enough to feel a little more confident, I returned from hiding.

"Shall we go?" I was hungry and wouldn't get anything to eat that night if I didn't control myself. After locking the front door, I turned, expecting to see him heading directly to the driver's seat. But he waited to walk me to his car, a far-from-new station wagon with fake wood on the sides. I liked it when he, the first man since Tim, opened my door for me.

A quick glance at his left hand startled me. No ring, but he had a pale band around his finger that implied he only recently stopped wearing his wedding ring. *Better be careful. Milt might be one of those professors we hear rumors about: B for a blowjob, A for all the way.* I bedded a professor if I liked him, but I didn't whore for grades. I wanted my degrees to mean something.

Needing to know more, a lot more, I listened intently to his small talk as we drove across town to the restaurant. I responded only when absolutely necessary to give me more time to process everything. Where was his wife on a Friday night? Out of town with the kids? Did he just want some nookie on the side? When we pulled into the Chez Nous parking lot, he hopped out quickly, opened my door for me, and gave me his hand to help me get out. No guy since Tim had treated me like this.

Chez Nous was, as the name suggested, a swanky French restaurant. I wasn't at all comfortable, but he didn't need to know it. Not yet. I needed to find out what exactly was his game? I didn't want to scare him off if he was on the level. He was sure trying to impress me. I just sat quietly and took it all in. On first dates, most men talk about themselves a lot, so that was easy.

Milt didn't simply order wine. He studied the list, asked the waiter several questions, incomprehensible to me, smelled the cork, swirled the wine in his glass, breathed in the bouquet, and only then did he taste it. I asked for cranberry juice.

Ordering our meals was simple compared to the wine. I ordered something expensive to see if he flinched. He didn't. I concluded that he wasn't just looking for a cheap lay.

When our meals were served, I saw the perfect opening to get an unguarded answer. Just as he put the second bite in his mouth, I asked, "So, how's your wife?"

Almost choking, he gathered himself. "Do you really want to know?"

"Trust me. I really do." *This ought to be good.*

"It's a long story."

"I've got all night." I shifted to a more comfortable position in my chair.

"Okay. I'll give you the abridged version."

"No need to leave out anything. I don't have other plans."

He took a swig of wine before starting. "I met Grace in grad school. She was a senior, majoring in art. We hit it off well and got married at the end of the summer after she graduated. She got pregnant on the honeymoon and put her talents to good use decorating our little apartment." He stopped to take a breath, then sipped his wine. "When I finished grad school and started teaching at the university, she got pregnant again, and again two years later."

"I suppose you had a little something to do with it."

He put his glass down before continuing. "I worked on my PhD, then getting a tenured job, and so forth while Grace raised the kids and managed the household. I moved up in the field, Grace got a larger house, and the kids got all the advantages we could afford plus those my affiliation with the university granted them." He looked deeply into my eyes.

"You're not wearing your ring for a reason." *Even it's just to integrate my denominator.*

"There's always a but, isn't there? A year ago, Grace informed me that she wasn't fulfilled in her role as wife and mother. I suggested, since the kids were all in school and didn't need her during the day, she take a part-time job, attend some classes she'd enjoy, do some painting, join Junior League, or do whatever would give her the most fulfillment."

"And she chose?" *Let me guess: an indoor sport?*

"To have an affair." His detached look suggested

she'd smashed his ego more than his heart.

"You're kidding." Some women I worked with got dissatisfied at home, had affairs, and got divorced, but weren't happy a few years later. Some tried to get their husbands back. I had better watch out for Grace. She might change her mind.

"Not in the least. She accused me of stifling her growth, of killing her spirit."

"And her tennis pro elevated her?" I raised my eyebrows.

"How did you know?"

"Did you forget that I'm a practicing statistician?"

"Sorry. Thanks for listening." He looked appreciative for letting him tell his tale of woe.

"How old are your children?" Kids can make a man more attractive.

His eyes sparkled. "My oldest is thirteen. Jessie was born when I was dissertating. Billy is ten and the baby, Sasha, is seven. She's the apple of my eye."

"Grace has the kids tonight?"

He nodded. "She picked them up right after school."

Cynthia warned me that divorced guys his age were often very confused, lonely, and needy. Better move slowly. Catching him on the rebound could be trouble.

"You seeing anyone else?"

"You're my first date since she left." He didn't flinch. He was telling the truth. "Even though she cheated on me, she expected more than half of everything, including custody of the kids. I didn't dare see you until the divorce was final, or she would've used you against me.

The decree came in the mail earlier this week."

"The day you tracked me down after class?"

"I didn't track you—Yes, I've been thinking about you a lot since seeing you on campus last semester before you burst into my office."

"Whoa! This is all very flattering, but please slow down."

"Okay, I will. Dessert?"

"No thanks. Have some if you'd like." I wanted to spend more time with him, but I usually did that in bed with a new guy. Sydney wasn't a complete substitute for a man, but Cynthia was right. I shouldn't bed Milt too soon. Such a quandary.

"It's early yet. Would you like to see the new Woody Allen film?"

"A comedy would be nice just now." *Perfect. Something light will extend the evening in a place where I won't rape him.*

"Check!"

eↄeↄ

Milt bought popcorn to munch on during the movie. I didn't eat any because it sticks in my teeth. My playful side hoped he'd put his hand on my thigh or higher, but I was glad he didn't. He was a perfect gentleman—too perfect for my liking, but I could change that.

He chattered about *Manhattan* while driving me home from the movie. "I liked it a lot more than his last film."

"Didn't like *Interiors*. Some don't consider it a Woody Allen film." *Pretty soon we'll exhaust my knowledge about Woody Allen. Better keep quiet.*

"Say, would you like a Manhattan?"

"I don't drink. Class tomorrow morning. Gotta get some sleep now."

I sat still in my seat when we arrived at my apartment. As expected, he walked around and opened my door for me. He even offered me his hand to help me get out of the car. I acted as if I didn't see it. I couldn't afford any physical contact yet. I could blow the whole thing.

I turned my head aside and pulled back far enough to see his face when he tried to kiss me at the door.

"Not until the third date." I wanted to give him a little goodnight kiss but thought better of it. *I need to make sure it's me he wants, not just a warm place to put it.*

"When will that be?" He frowned like a spoiled child not getting what he wants.

"It depends on how the second one goes. It might be never."

"Let's take in a Broadway show tomorrow night."

"I'll be too tired." He was moving too fast, but it was nice having someone hot for me.

"A Sunday matinee?"

He must be even hornier than I thought. "No. But I'll see you the next Saturday you don't have the kids."

"Two weeks from tomorrow, it is."

I pushed the door open and shut it behind me so fast he didn't have time to react. I reclined on the couch in my best Garbo imitation and basked in exuberance because a man really—I mean, really—wanted me.

CHAPTER 6

Standardizing My Deviates

Milt crossed my path numerous times over the next two weeks. I acted coy by avoiding the office and pretending I didn't notice him or engaging a classmate in conversation when I saw him coming, but it wasn't easy. He seemed to pop up every time I was in the hallway, especially after class.

"Hello, Professor Hay." I felt uncomfortable talking with him where we might be seen by other students or faculty. Keeping my emotions under control in private was hard enough.

Before speaking to me, he nervously scanned the hallway, first to his left, then the right to make sure we were alone. "Hello, Tookie," he said, "I got us tickets for *Evita*. I'll pick you up at five-thirty Saturday, and we'll have a leisurely dinner in the city before the show."

"You've got to be more careful." I feared a scandal would hurt Milt professionally and kill my chances mat-rimonially. "Be on your way before someone sees us." I nudged him opposite the direction I was going before anyone else came along.

Being invited to a Broadway show, especially a hit musical, was an ego boost. Milt's willingness to spend so much just for the pleasure of my company told me he was serious. He might even have been as smitten as I was.

I wanted to show Milt I could play the part of a department head's wife, but I didn't think I had anything appropriate to wear—until I flipped through the few dresses in my closet. Stuffed in the corner, I found the emerald green beaded dress Jack bought me to play the flapper gun moll at his trade show.

Wearing sexy clothes was awkward for me. Misleading men to think of me as some sort of sex goddess made me feel like a fraud. However, landing Milt required me to get out of my comfort zone, way out. I dyed an inexpensive pair of dressy flats to match the dress, yielding me a designer outfit at negligible cost. Fortunately for me, girls could get away with forgoing heels in New York. With all that walking, it was too easy to twist an ankle, and running to catch a bus would be downright dangerous. Work, school, and date preparations had kept me so busy I had little opportunity to fret. All of a sudden, the night of my big date was on me. When I realized it was almost time for Milt to pick me up, butterflies attacked my stomach with a vengeance. Rebrushing my hair and adjusting my pantyhose to look well put together filled the remaining minutes.

Knock, knock.

Be calm. "Come in. It's unlocked." I'd left the door

ajar and positioned a mirror so I could see his reaction.

"Oh, T—Tookie, I guess I'm a little early, but—" He never stuttered, nor was he ever at a loss for words, but he was stunned by what he saw.

"Do you like it?" I spun to give him a better rear view. In the mirror, I noticed his jaw drop. "I'm ready now."

"I'll s—say you're ready. Y—You'd fit in at the Oscars. I always th—thought you were good looking, but w—wow!" He wiped the drool off his lips when he thought he was out of view.

He uncharacteristically babbled as we drove to the station, rode the train to the city, and took a cab to an up-scale restaurant in the Theater District. There, he helped me out of the cab and looked around to see if anyone important was nearby before paying the driver. He bent his arm for me to hold and promenaded me to the maître d's station as if we were royalty.

"Reservations for Hay, table for two." He slipped him a five.

Rolling his eyes so Milt couldn't see him, the maître d' said, "Come this way."

Milt puffed out his chest and strutted like a pigeon, and we zig-zagged our way past numerous diners to get to our table. Milt tilted his head back just enough to look snobbish but not enough not to be able to see everyone he passed. For once, I was dressed more stylishly than most of the other women. I didn't have to swing my ass to make the beaded fringe sway. It did that on its own. The motion caught the attention of men across the room.

Some even stole glances at me as we passed.

His behavior was even worse during *Evita*. At intermission, he made a point of walking me to the lobby to "get some air," but the way he paraded me through the crowd told me he was showing me off. His head darted from side to side as he charted his course past who he thought were the most important people. It was his way of saying, "Look at me now, Grace." He was so funny, I hardly kept a straight face. The affected look he put on his face was surely humorous to those who bothered to look at him.

After the play, he took me to Lindy's to show off again. Milt must have plotted a course that, at one point or another, took us past every table at least once. I doubted anyone in any of the places knew him, but it sure gave him a thrill seeing the looks I got him. It's a wonder he had any buttons left on his shirt. Feeling so self-conscious playing such a glamorous role, I struggled to keep the charade going but managed somehow until it was time for him to drop me off.

"Thank you for a wonderful evening, Milt." He tried to kiss me, but I didn't dare let him because my resistance was so low. I pushed my palms against his chest and stepped back, smiling with the demure grin I had seen movie actresses use, saying, "Let me know what plans you make for our next date." Then I closed the door behind me.

Off came the dress, nylons, and panties for my date with Sydney. Fantasizing he was Milt intensified my reactions and got me through the night.

Milt's next kid-free weekend fell on homecoming. I didn't want to wait two weeks to spend time with him again but knew controlling my feelings around him would be a challenge. So, I arranged for us to meet off-campus at Harvest Moon, an out-of-the-way sandwich shop, for a quick supper before our Wednesday night classes. It wasn't a date, not really. We just used the time to plan our homecoming weekend. I didn't mind being rushed because that gave me bonus time with him. And I was protected from myself because I didn't have the time or place to jump him.

Milt had to participate in several homecoming events, but none during the football game. I volunteered to organize a Stats Department section and talked several students and faculty members into attending. One evening right after work, I dropped into the office to coordinate some details with Pam, the department secretary who'd befriended me during my undergraduate days.

Bam! It sounded like a heavy book slammed against a desk or the floor.

"If you want better test scores, do more homework," Milt shouted.

"You're being unfair," whined a petite coed as she stormed out of his office.

"Better keep clear of him until his mood passes," Pam said. "I'll ask him how many tickets he needs later."

I'd never known him to lose his cool before, but thought I'd have been just as irritated by a grade whore demanding a higher mark.

I got the tickets to the football game for the department and, surprise, Milt's seat was on my right. We came separately and left separately. I didn't hold his hand or anything but "accidentally" brushed his inner thigh when I stood up to cheer. Surprisingly, our team scored several times, giving me opportunities to perfect my move. Sometimes, when the others were distracted by what was happening on the field, I'd whisper things like, "What color garter belt do you prefer?" in his ear, in the huskiest voice I could manage, but not loud enough for him to make out exactly what I said. A couple of times it was necessary to admonish him with a look when he unwisely rested his hand on my highly sensitive inner thigh. At game's end, I waited for him to leave and immediately headed in the opposite direction.

At home, I took a cold shower instead of having a Sydney session in order to be fully charged for whatever might happen after dinner. Shortly after dark, Milt dropped by my apartment to take me to a quiet, romantic place a few miles outside of town away from prying eyes. In sharp contrast to our theater date, he didn't strut, and we both dressed casually in earth tones to be as inconspicuous as possible.

"How was your meal?" he asked after the main course. This being our third date, he probably expected a good night kiss and, hopefully, wanted more.

"Excellent, but I'm tired from the day's activities. Can I give you a rain check for the rest of the date? I'll make it up to you. Promise." *You'll be surprised by what I give you.*

He looked like a little boy whose puppy had died. "Okay."

When we got to my apartment, I didn't dally getting out of his car and to my door. Milt followed close behind. I unlocked and breezed in before he could make a move, but left the door ajar. He followed me in, his pout turning to a smile, probably because he was thinking he'd finally get his promised kiss.

"Close the door, please. I don't like to be kissed goodnight with neighbors watching me."

He was getting the kiss. That much I'd decided. But how much more was up in the air. I wanted him badly but didn't want him to think I wasn't wife material. I had cleaned my apartment and put a bouquet of fall flowers on the mantle for scent, just in case.

Ambivalence ruled. I uncharacteristically let him take the lead and would go where he led me, if anywhere. He wasted no time.

Not bad. I wanted more and kissed him back. He continued. I encouraged him with tiny moans when I enjoyed what he did. He led me to the couch, and I gave him no resistance. I only stopped him once, when he neglected my breasts and prematurely reached up the bottom of my dress.

"Please," I said, guiding his hand back to my bead-covered breast.

I scorched quickly—not having a man for several weeks does that to me. Combining horniness with falling in love is a lethal combination. I craved skin-on-skin contact, and my breasts hungered to be massaged, licked, sucked, bitten, and twirled desperately but, even un-zipped, my dress would still be in the way. My desires and emotions outstripped my brain.

I turned my back to him, and he took the hint by un-zipping me all the way down to my waist. Turning to face him, I pressed my burning lips tight to his, sucking in his plunging tongue, fighting my desire to bite him. Sizzling, I stood so he could finish what he had started. Already unzipped, I reached for the ceiling. He pulled my dress up, over my head, and off, leaving me in a slip, bra, panty hose, and panties that all needed to be removed. I didn't mind his rustiness. He was supposed to be out of practice. He easily shed me of my slip and unhooked my bra, toss-ing it somewhere. He tended my aroused breasts well enough, but he was impatient to ride me. I worked to keep him on task. Even when he had me down to my pan-tyhose, I still could've stopped him, but my body wasn't considering any reason or resolve.

"Are you sure you really want me, Milt? I don't want a one-night stand." I panted, and not just because I was so horny.

"I want you more than anything, now and forever." He panted even more than I did.

I led him to my playroom where we'd be more com-fortable on my bed. I wrapped my lips around his, stab-bing my tongue down his throat. He struggled with my pantyhose.

"I'll get them." I ducked into my bathroom where I also inserted a sponge to be doubly safe. I wanted to fin-ish grad school and wouldn't be accused of trapping him in a shotgun marriage if my IUD failed again.

Returning completely naked, Milt, in just his skivvies, looked me up and down, smiling and let out a wolf whistle.

I felt like I was dripping on the floor I was so aroused.

He led me by the hand to the bed. He was awkward and gave me the impression he hadn't been with many women before Grace, who probably wasn't very adventurous—at least with him.

"Please don't take advantage of me, Milt. I'll do anything to make you happy, provided you're serious about me."

"I couldn't be more serious, Tookie." He tore off his boxers, then gently spread my legs and lifted my knees.

I held back from pulling him into me, not wanting him to think I was an old hand at this.

It took a lot of self-control, not grabbing hold of Milt Minor, while he took three tries to plug himself into my well lubricated love canal.

It pained me not to taste him, but it was imperative for him not to know how experienced I was. A couple of pleasant—make that three—goes missionary style, and we both fell contented into deep sleep.

ⱷⱷⱷ

In the morning, I awoke to the sound of a closing door. *Shit. Did he get up and leave without saying good-bye?* I raced to the living room picture window to watch him pull out, but I couldn't see his car. Nothing moved in the lot. His car wasn't parked where he left it the night before. I shouldn't have let him fuck me so soon. *Cynthia was right. I've lost him already.*

Scrraaape. A chair slid across the linoleum floor.

I dashed to the kitchen.

"How do you like your coffee?" The wonderfully pleasant aroma of the bitter-tasting liquid wafted into my nose just as his voice caressed my ears.

Milt was unloading bagels from a bag. The Sunday *Times* lay on the table.

"I don't." My body was so confused, it didn't know how to react.

He looked up from the coffee and bagels to see me in my full glory and smiled. "Forget these bagels. I see what I'm going to have."

"We need to talk." My mood shifted from despair, hurt, and anger through confusion to happiness in less time than a dirty thought took to traverse his synapses. The abrupt jolts, first downward, then upward, convulsed my emotions and tied my stomach into knots.

He pushed the chair next to him back and patted it. "Please sit down, dear." He wouldn't have known my chair—the one I usually use—was opposite his.

"Not like this." Stark naked, I felt cold and defense-less while he ogled me. I was probably insecure after thinking he'd deserted me. I didn't previously know it was possible, but I felt like he was undressing me with his eyes.

"I like you like this," he said, shifting his vision between the two places I covered with my hands.

I dashed to my room and threw on a white terrycloth bathrobe and stepped into my white fuzzy slippers.

Milt slid a coffee toward me on my return.

I got a small glass out of the cupboard, saying, "Don't like the stuff," and poured myself a glass of OJ. Milt slid the bag of bagels in my direction. I pulled out a blueberry one, cut it in half—the pre-slicer never cuts all the way through—and popped it into the toaster. I felt confident enough to talk about *us* after I had smeared cream cheese on it and sat in my usual place. "I feel very vulnerable right now. I didn't intend to sleep with you last night. It's much too early in our relationship." I didn't shake, but I nearly did because I thought I'd blown my chances with him.

He looked me straight into my eyes and said, "I'm glad we did. I love you, and I think you love me. Nothing else matters."

"I'm afraid you won't respect me. My emotions took control last night."

Milt walked around the table, hugged me from behind, and kissed my neck. "I've been looking forward to being with you since seeing you on campus last term. What would you like to do today?"

"I need to be cuddled right now."

We spent the rest of the morning in bed. He had to appear on campus in the afternoon for more homecoming activities. Afterward, he dropped by on the way to pick up his kids. "Let's make next time as special as this one."

"Will you take me to The Point on Upper Saranac

Lake? I want you to myself the whole weekend. I didn't intend to have sex with you this soon." I needed him to invest as much emotionally in me as I had in him. Spending a long weekend together without distractions should help.

"Really?"

That I wanted to go to such an exclusive place probably surprised him. "We can go boating and canoeing on the lake," I said. "We can make s'mores in the campfire or just stay in our room by the fireplace. We can even have our meals in bed."

Perhaps thinking about what I'd give him that weekend, he smiled broadly. "I'm a romantic at heart. I'll book it."

"Get your tux cleaned for Saturday night dinner. Should I bring the green dress?"

"All you'll need is fresh underwear for the trip home."

"Be careful what you ask for. I'll only take my toiletries kit. I'll put on clean underwear after showering Friday morning, fold them neatly into a drawer after arriving at The Point, and put them back on before checking out if that's what you want."

After pondering my offer a few seconds, he said, "On second thought, I may want to show you off."

∽∂∾

He made up an excuse why Grace had to pick up the kids from school, and she bought it. We both called in sick and left for The Point as soon as the kids caught their school bus Friday morning.

"This isn't the way," I said, thinking my absent-minded professor had taken a wrong turn.

"Yes, it is," he said, completely nonchalant with a smug look on his face.

I turned my back to him. "This's the way to the airport, not upstate New York." I have little patience with men who refuse to admit they've made a wrong turn. I drummed my fingers on his station wagon's dashboard.

"That's right." He smiled like a smartass who thought he was right when he wasn't.

When he took the airport exit, I got more irritated, even more so when he parked in the general aviation lot. When he opened my door, I sat there unmoving.

"What're you doing?" I asked. He was exasperating me by wasting time we could be on a mini-vacation.

"Surprise. I booked a charter, so we'll get there earlier."

I kissed him on the cheek. "Thank you." I felt ashamed for doubting him.

✂∾✂∾

The Point's shuttle driver dropped us off at the main lodge of the secluded, posh Adirondack great camp. While we registered, employees lugged our suitcases to our room above the boathouse, my choice. Milt wanted the Mohawk, the Rockefellers' master bedroom, but spoiled me further by letting me have my way. We joined eight other visitors for lunch on the veranda before retiring to our room to freshen up. We decided we'd take out one of the classic mahogany boats after unpacking and exploring our quarters.

The huge bed sat in the center of the room like a medieval queen's, giving me breathtakingly beautiful vistas of the lake on three sides. The suite, located above the boats docked directly underneath us, allowed a good view of them coming and going. The open headboard didn't block the heat from the large granite fireplace a few paces behind it.

"Put on your sneakers, Tooks, while I brush my teeth." He retreated into the bathroom, leaving the door open.

I saw my chance to thank Milt for the weekend he was giving me. I slunk into the bathroom and silently dropped to my knees in front of him. I unbuckled his belt, unzipped his fly, and opened his trousers, letting them drop to the floor.

"Huh." He couldn't form words with his mouth full of toothpaste.

"Shhhsh. Relax, or I'll lose my nerve." I warmed up little Milt through the opening in his boxers and pulled them down before he interrupted me. I gave him my plain vanilla treatment, not wanting to shock him with my experience, but probably better than what Grace ever gave him.

"Wow." He panted and took a deep breath. "I don't know what to say."

"Thank you will do. If you don't like it, I won't do it again."

He kissed me. "Thank you, Tookie. Thank you. Thank you." He flopped on the bed. "I like it very much. I had no idea it could feel so good."

"I liked giving it to you. The book said I would, but I wasn't so sure. Did I do it right?"

჻

We didn't leave the room until the antique Swiss cuckoo clock on the wall signaled it was time for the formal dinner the next night. I did everything he asked me to do. Nothing exotic at all. Just nice. I did insist on being a cowgirl sometimes. I'd have to think of a way to integrate some less common, but very pleasurable, techniques into our lovemaking without revealing how many miles were on my odometer. Having a false sense of privacy in the boathouse—he didn't want others hearing us make love—it didn't bother him when I vocalized considerably louder than I had in my apartment with paper-thin walls.

The looks I got from other guests when he paraded me to dinner told me they'd taken out boats that afternoon. Silly Milt thought the other men were envious of him for my looks.

His face turned beet red when he looked at his steak. "This is burned. I ordered rare." Milt's filet wasn't exactly right, but not so bad I wouldn't have eaten it without complaint.

"I'm sorry, sir. I'll get you another." The waiter dashed off to the kitchen with the offending beef while diners at other tables rolled their eyes or shook their heads.

The manager approached our table with a bottle of burgundy cradled in his arm. "Would you like a glass of 1971 Grand Cru, sir? We've too little left to put it out for everyone. It's very special if you've never had it."

Milt's frown turned to curiosity. "Yes. I've not been able to find it anywhere." He thought of himself as something of an expert on wines.

The manager poured him a generous portion and looked at me.

I put my hand over my glass and shook my head.

Milt received more stares that night than I did, but no one approached us when we were standing on the veranda after dinner or any other time the rest of the weekend. Our mini-vacation went smoothly after that. We cooed like lovebirds in our nest up in the boathouse and all the way home.

We were in our getting-to-know-each-other-better phase. We decided to wait until we'd dated for six months before introducing me to his kids. We needed to deal with them very carefully because children are the single largest factor in second marriages failing. In the meantime, we frolicked, doing all manner of things on alternate weekends. I focused on my schoolwork the weekends he had the kids. Things went very smoothly for us as we very much enjoyed each other's company, and he couldn't get enough of me.

The time to meet his children finally came in March. I expected them to take to me because kids usually do. Milt decided to have me over to start a new family tradition.

Milt and his progeny had assembled in his cozy family room after dinner. "Kids, I told you we were going to have a special guest tonight, and here she is. This is my special friend, Miss Woodstream." The kids looked skeptical.

My stomach tensed, but I faked being at ease. "Hi, guys."

Sasha, the baby at seven, spoke first: "Are you going to be our new mother?"

Jessie, the oldest at thirteen, screwed her face tightly saying, "We already have a mother."

"You already have a mother and don't need me to be one, too, do you?"

"I thought tonight was supposed to be Game Night," said Billy, the middle child, looking disappointed.

"And so it is," Milt jumped in. "Which one do we want to play first? How about Parcheesi?"

"Yeah," the two younger kids shouted while Jessie smirked disapproval.

"Will you be my partner?" Sasha asked.

"Of course. Do you know how to play Parcheesi?"

"No."

"I'll show you."

Sasha pushed her chair against mine at the poker table.

It was tense at first, but no disaster. Things weren't

exactly rosy, but warmer than an armed truce. Two weeks later, it was a different situation. I looked forward to Game Night, hopeful to build on what had been established last time. It could serve as a foundation upon which the children and I would build good relationships.

"Mom said you aren't a nice person, and I should stay away from you," said Sasha with a look of sadness on her face.

I tried to hug her, but she pulled away.

"You're a slut," Jessie said. "You're taking Dad away from Mom."

I didn't know what the little bitch wanted from me. I just wanted to be her friend, not a role model.

Milt backhanded her. "Go to your room. Now!"

Jessie stormed away, slamming her bedroom door behind her.

Billy stood up, looking defiant. "I don't know what slut means, but Mom told our friends' moms not to let them play with us when you're here. I want my friends to come over."

Seeing this was something Milt had to handle by himself. I excused myself and drove home, crying all the way. He was right about one thing. Grace was a bitch. She surely orchestrated this to make Milt's life miserable. I resolved to back away for a while and not see him when he had the children.

⨯⨯⨯

Things went smoothly between us for the next year,

with him getting increasingly dependent on me. In a way, Grace had done me a favor. With eleven days between our weekends together, Milt climbed the walls with desire. He didn't get the chance to get bored and couldn't pressure me to move in before we married. After the kids were in bed the Saturday nights he had them, I treated him to phone sex. That was great fun. I got him to do all sorts of strange things. As for myself, on other nights I had Sydney, who was always available and didn't pout if I ignored him for extended periods.

Things were perfect in many ways. I had most of my time free to do my coursework and visit with girlfriends. Our relationship didn't interfere with my work or school. I enjoyed sex with Milt and didn't see him often enough to get bored. Never before had a man wanted me so badly every time we were together. I left sex books lying about my apartment to give him the impression I was studying new techniques as I slowly ratcheted up my game. I marked pages for him but didn't say anything. He read them, though. I know because he tried the new positions out on me.

Milt flared at me a few times, like he had at the waiter and Jessie, but he quickly apologized. I sensed when I was irritating him and curbed my tongue—most of the time. My biological clock napped restlessly because his kids' attitudes put marriage on hold. I could wait a few years. My daughter wasn't going to be a fatherless bastard.

Having Milt for a couple of courses created challenges and opportunities. The semesters I was in his classes, he shifted his office hours to end an hour and a half before class started. I took off work a little early on those days to have "dinner" with him in the privacy of his office. The intrigue and the possibility someone might walk in on us excited me. As much fun as this was, it didn't make up for not knowing if anything was going to come of my relationship with Milt.

How much longer would I have to wait to have and hold a daughter of my own?

CHAPTER 7

My Trouble with Speedos

Summers were a different story for Milt and me. His research grant sent him to Italy in our first year of dating because he'd committed to that before we became an item. I planned our second summer together before he could commit to anything foolish that would take him away from me. Finishing my masters in June gave me much more freedom for the summer of 1981. With no more classes to fill my evenings and weekends, or homework and papers to eat up my remaining free time, I finally had time available to plan a great vacation. With ample banked vacation time, where to have Milt take me was the question.

I looked forward to that vacation for an entire year. Even though I used a project from work for my thesis, writing it up in the school's format stole a lot of my time and effort and required a couple of rewrites. Thoughts of lounging about, catching up on my trash reading, sleeping in, and being waited upon kept me going until it was time to leave. We decided on a place within driving range to relieve us from the stresses of catching a plane or dealing with weather delays. Milt agreed, a rustic cabin at a small, exclusive retreat on a New Hampshire lake resort would fit the bill perfectly.

The first week was uneventful, exactly what I needed. But a hot guy, who proved to be trouble, arrived in the middle of our stay. He first appeared at the lake while I sat in a deck chair on a humid, sunny day in the tiny piece of shade under the lone apple tree at the rear edge of the beach, reading the latest John MacDonald novel. Why he picked me, with 96 SPF sunscreen slathered an inch-thick all over my body, was a mystery.

I was one of the minority of American women who preferred men in Speedos—providing they had the build for them, and he did. Apparently, women, who didn't like their men in Speedos, felt slighted when the objects of their affections displayed more than a passing interest in others in full view of everyone within eyeshot. I, on the other hand, feasted—if only visually most of the time—on seeing his interest in full bloom masked by only a thin layer of Spandex, regardless of whom it was complimenting.

"How do you like *Free Fall in Crimson*, eh?" asked a male I hadn't heard before.

My broad-brimmed straw hat blocked my view, and I didn't want to look too interested by lifting my head up from my book. I liked the sound of his smooth baritone voice and his Canadian accent. "And you are?"

"Josh. The guy you've been waiting for all afternoon."

I lowered my book and looked up at him. "Not as well as his last one," I said, answering his first question.

He puffed out his chest. "Stay with it. It gets better."

"Did you just arrive? I haven't noticed you before." My early-teen-like voice sounded more silly than sexy to me.

"Just this morning. Go for drinks later?"

Milt opened the gate and walked across the sand toward me. He'd pass the bar soon and would be able to see me—and Josh. Wanting to head off a nasty confrontation, I demurred. "Can't this trip."

I loved flirting when nothing could come of it. Finally, in my prime, I savored the attention boys denied me in high school and college. I didn't want flings with most of them, just ego boosts.

Seeing me—and Josh—Milt sped up.

I flicked at Josh with the back of my hand. "Better go now."

He saw my eyes following Milt. "You married or something?"

"Or something, but I plan on marrying him some day." I refocused my attention to my book, and Josh turned wistfully away.

Milt stretched himself to full height and towered over me, with his neck veins bulging and nostrils flared. "Who's that guy?"

"Just someone new who arrived today."

"It looked like he was hitting on you."

I glared at him. "You think I'm so ugly men never hit on me?"

He looked annoyed. "If I thought that, I wouldn't worry, would I?"

"I'll take that as a compliment since you give me so few of them." Sometimes, I said things just to fluster men. It was fun to see them react.

"From my vantage point, it looked like you were hitting on him."

"You don't have any claims on me." I wiggled the naked ring finger of my left hand. "I can't even remember the last time you mentioned marriage."

"You know well enough I'd gladly marry you today if my kids weren't such a problem."

My stomach didn't churn this time. Had I stopped worrying about losing him?

"Yeah, Yeah, Yeah." *Is this relationship slipping away, too? But I've invested so much in it.*

Milt said, "I'm going back to the room," and left.

As soon as he was out of sight, Josh sidled up to my shaded chaise lounge again.

I slowly ran my fingers up and down his butt while watching his front for a reaction. "None of my boyfriends wore Speedos. I've always wondered what they felt like." *Dry.*

Touching the texture of his Speedo and seeing his instantaneous erection stretch the fabric to its limit brought to mind a youthful conquest. During rare summer breaks between classes when in my early twenties, I sometimes went to the Jersey shore in the late afternoon or on weekends with the more adventurous girls from work. We always picked a spot to display ourselves to single young men. One particular evening was indelibly etched on my memory…

❧❧❧

"Here's the deal," said Jackie, who worked in accounts receivable and always made sure she got her fair share of whatever was being distributed. "We each put in five dollars, and the first to get a meat thermometer to pop, gets the pot to pay for a motel room."

"What about the rest of the girls?" asked Sybil, the pretty blonde Jersey girl who taught me how to pick up men at bars. "I'm not the only one who'll need a room."

"You'll have to wait your turn," Jackie responded. "We each get the room for an hour in the order we need one."

"When does the timer start?" I asked to clarify things. "With the first sign of desire or the first move toward the room?"

"When one of us asks you for the room key with a guy in hand," said Jackie.

Seeing me in my swim suit, the others were sure I wouldn't need the room as soon as they would, if ever. I agreed about the swim suit part, but thought otherwise about spending the night dickless and played along to be part of the group.

"I'll make it fairer by giving everyone else a head start," said Sybil. "Give me your five bucks, and I'll get the key."

We handed her our money and took full advantage of her absence by strutting past a couple of guys who appeared to be looking for a place to put their blankets down. Before long, my thick thighs and I were alone on my blanket holding the key. I'd put myself at a tremendous disadvantage in letting the guys get their first impression of me by seeing my least attractive features on full display.

As the sun lowered in the sky, I got moist watching a French Canadian whose red Speedo hid nothing. When he walked into the waves, it was the right time to make my move.

I scurried into the surf and made my way toward him, but waited until his skimpy suit was submerged to get close.

"Hi," I said, unable to think of something witty that wouldn't scare him away.

"Come here often?" he responded in what I'd correctly assumed would be a French Canadian accent. Americans and English-speaking Canadians seldom wore those things.

"Only when I see a man fill out a Speedo as well as you do."

He stammered, "Uh…uh… you have beautiful hair," and edged carefully out into deeper water as if he was unaccustomed to being pursued by a woman with intentions.

"Thanks," I said, following him. "Do you have plans for the evening?"

His head swiveled around as if he was looking for a rescuer. "Nothing specific."

Sliding my hand into the front of his tight trunks was a challenge.

He flinched.

Oooh. No jock strap. "Hold still. You'll enjoy this more."

He smiled. Being considerably taller, he held me by the shoulders to keep the waves from pushing us apart.

Not enough room in there to do anything. Better roll it down.

"Ahhhh." He looked pleasantly surprised when I fondled his freed package like one massages a child's feet after removing her shoes.

"Stand still." After a few strokes and tickles, he throbbed in my hand, ready to rock my roll. *Should I risk not having him for the evening by whacking him off now?*

"There's a perfect place under the boardwalk." Rolling his Speedo back up was more difficult than rolling it down, but I soon had his desire for me covered, mostly.

"Race you to your blanket," he said, lust dripping from every pore.

"Last one there eats the other."

He ran. I walked. The memory of the fun I had that night brought me back to the opportunity at hand.

❦

With Milt around, I had to be more careful with Josh than I had been with the Canuck. Josh snapped to attention as I'd hoped he would and blushed, probably because his desire for me was so noticeable.

"Would you like a drink now?"

"If you insist." I put down my book and sashayed over to the beachside bar with him. He drank an imported beer, and I had my usual cranberry juice. It didn't take long for Milt to reappear—angrier than when he left.

I whispered, "Leave now, or he'll make a scene."

Josh took the hint. "Later."

"I saw you flirting with that guy again." In a rage, Milt threw my cranberry juice in my face and on my now psychedelic white blouse that protected me from another round of skin cancer.

The bartender froze in disbelief, and the couple standing at the bar whispered low enough not to be heard. Apparently shocked by his failure to control his emotions, Milt stomped away.

Stunned, I slowly wiped my face and gathered my composure enough to walk back to the room. After cleaning my blouse in the sink the best I could, I stepped into the shower.

Milt had been angry with other people, and he swatted one of his kids, but he'd never come close to doing anything physical toward me. When he entered the bathroom, I shuddered, something I'd never done before.

"I'm terribly sorry, Tookie," he said when I turned the water off. "You know I'm not normally a jealous person, but I can't bear the thought of losing you." He tried to touch me, but I slapped his hand away.

"I don't think I should give you another chance."

Fear of Milt's rage overcame me for the first time. I put on a bathrobe for protection.

He looked pathetic as he pleaded, "Please tell me what I can do to make it up to you."

He was so penitent, my fear diminished, but my anger rose. "There's no way for you to make up for it. Do anything like that again, and you're history."

For dinner, I normally ordered chicken or something equally inexpensive. That night, Milt insisted I have something fancier. He was quite attentive. Things seemed to have been smoothed over until Josh walked past the table, and I winked at him. *Damn it, Milt saw me.* I waited for him to say something, but he didn't. He gave me the silent treatment.

"Cat got your tongue? You're never quiet this long." I touched his hand.

He pulled away. "I don't have anything to say."

"I'm going back to the room. You can stay here and sulk if you want."

I read, sitting up in bed, engrossed in my book. I left the door unlocked in case I fell asleep. I must have dozed off.

Smack. "Oww!" My face burned. *Damn, that hurts.*

It was Milt, and he smelled of booze. I needed to get away from him as quickly as possible. I rolled off the bed and ran to the bathroom, locking the door behind me. In the mirror, I saw the imprint of his fingers on my cheek. "You bastard. You hit me for the last time."

Knock. Knock. "I'm sorry, Tookie. I lost my head. I'll never do it again."

"Go away. I don't wanna see you. Find yourself another place to sleep."

After the door latch clicked, signaling his departure, I emerged from the sanctuary of the bathroom to bolt the room door, so he couldn't get back in. Holding an ice cube to my cheek numbed the sting and calmed my shaking, but not my stomach. Safe for now, I dialed the phone. "Do you have a minute, Evelyn?"

"Where are you? I thought you were on vacation. What's wrong?"

"What makes you think something is wrong?"

"I hear it in your voice, and you never call when you're away on a tryst."

"Don't worry. I'm safe now." I held a plastic bag full of ice to my cheek that burned again after the first cube had had melted. "He's locked out of the room and always cools off once he realizes what he's done."

"Always? Has he done this before?"

"Never. I flirted with a Canadian in a Speedo."

"You and those darned Speedos. Won't you ever learn?"

"Learn what?"

"To leave guys with Speedos alone. They're no good for you, and neither is Milt. Leave him before he hurts you seriously."

"He's always so contrite." The ice was finally working.

"I better come pick you up. Give me directions."

"No need. You wouldn't get here till tomorrow morning, and that's if you drove all night. I'll be okay."

Evelyn always exaggerated the seriousness of things.

"Do you want to be crowned Miss Denial of 1981? Don't call me when they take you away in an ambulance."

I slept soundly until morning.

Knock. Knock.

"Who's there?"

"Gifts for you," came from a female voice on the other side of the door.

"Just a minute." I put on a robe before opening the door even though I had pajamas on. I didn't feel safe enough to sleep naked in case he burst his way in.

"Where would you like them?" She looked for a place to put a large, expensive basket of fruit and a large box of chocolates.

"Is there a card?"

As she handed it to me, I pointed to where she should put the fruit and made a mental note to increase our tip. I opened the card, hoping it was from Josh. They were from Milt, begging my forgiveness. I scribbled a note, "I don't want to see or hear from you right now. Don't push me or we leave today," and handed it to the girl. "Please deliver this to the man who sent this stuff. The front desk will know where he is."

He never hit me again, but he raged often. Almost all of his outbursts were the result of me pushing his buttons. One of my bad qualities was detecting men's vulnerabilities and poking them in their weak spots. Maybe I had a sadomasochistic streak. Other men had reacted negatively, but they didn't hit me. Milt wasn't violent unless I provoked him. It was my fault but I no longer cared.

Milt knew to keep his distance and met me for lunch at the maître d's stand.

"We'd like a quiet table in the corner."

The maître d' motioned us to follow him. "This way."

As soon as we placed or orders, Milt started in. "I really can't bear—"

"Can it, Milt. This is how it's gonna be." *I can't stand being near you anymore.*

"But, but—"

"No buts. You're going to stay in a different room. I'll pack your bags and call a bellboy to deliver them to you. We'll have meals together if you want. Beyond that, I don't know. I don't want you even looking in my direction when we're not together. What I do is my business. We're not married or even making plans. Remember?"

He sat uncomfortably silent.

"If I wanna fuck somebody else, it's my business. As it happens, I don't have any intentions in that regard, no matter what you may think. When we get back home, we're reassessing our relationship. Got it?"

He nodded.

Not wanting hassles from Milt, Josh, or any other male the rest of the stay, I donned my swimming suit before sitting by the lake to read instead of the cute blouse and clamdiggers I'd been wearing. This trip ended without me giving in to sex, thank you very much.

The journey home wasn't pleasant. I read in the

backseat while Milt drove, and I played the radio too loudly to hear him when I was at the wheel.

Back at home, I focused on work and ignored Milt. Getting my master's degree would make me eligible for a significant promotion I wanted. The increased pay would make life easier, and the title would gain me more respect. Many people, men and women alike, assumed someone with a little-girl voice such as mine was a junior person with little expertise. Perhaps the advanced degree would help me overcome that bias. The morning after my last final exams forever, my clock ticked so loudly I could no longer ignore it.

Milt and I had devolved into a one-date per weekend-without-the-kids pattern and a lot less sex. Neither of us was happy with the relationship, but it was more convenient than looking for someone else. Christmas holidays away from my scattered family were always hard, especially so when my boyfriend was tied up so much with his family's affairs. We never did develop a strategy for dealing with his children.

Being the only non-drinker at the New Year's Eve party we attended gave me a lot of time to ponder my situation. As the New Year rang in, I decided to ring Milt out, but I waited until he called me a few days later to tell him we were through.

"Hi, Took. *Reds* is playing on campus this weekend. Everybody's talking about it."

He's making it easy. The thought of being trapped for three hours in a room full of commie wannabes sickens me. "I'll pass." I probably sounded as nauseated as I felt.

"What would you like to do?" He sounded desperate.

"Nothing." I tried to sound as cold as I felt about him.

Not getting my hint as usual, he perked up a bit. "That's okay. We can call out for pizza."

"You're being thick. I don't wanna do anything with you ever again."

"If it's anything I've done, I can change," he begged.

"It's over, Milt." *Click.* I couldn't handle confrontation, and this was dragging on too long.

Going through graduation was out. I'd finished all the requirements for my masters before Christmas break and had looked forward to going through the ceremony, but Milt would be the one who would turn my hood and hand me my diploma. No way could I have stood that. The only times I ever returned to campus after that were when I knew he was in class or away at a conference.

Jackson and Jackson passed me over for the promotion in favor of a couple of less experienced, but more politically astute, men—office politics were never my strong suit.

My boss was so arrogant about it, I sent out resumes that very day. Getting no immediate responses, I hung on longer than I planned. When offers trickled in spring 1982, I took the best one, a position with a large multi-national firm I knew I'd love working for.

Suing Jackson and Jackson for sex discrimination wasn't worth the effort. Responding to their lawyers' legal maneuvers would have cost me more than I could afford, and my stomach churned every time I got a letter from them. So, after being bullied this way, I settled for a measly thousand bucks. At least I liked my new job analyzing clinical data to present to the government as part of the drug approval process.

My brilliant academician didn't work out, and my clock ticked incessantly. I was way overdue for something good, but would I get it?

CHAPTER 8

Nathaniel

I husband-hunted most of 1982, seldom seeing—or sleeping with—anyone more than a few times. I couldn't afford to waste my time with guys not interested in fatherhood or who weren't husband material. My loudly ticking biological clock constantly reminded me I needed a man, but not just any man. He had to be reliable and in it for the long run. Most of the men in my age bracket who were still single were very much into themselves. But these self-absorbed jerks still got all the rumpy-pumpy they wanted—and from younger, more nubile women than me.

When I was on a dating drought, Tim came to mind. He was definitely husband and father material, even if he was boring. At least he loved me. A quick call to my brother, Daniel, who communicated with one of Tim's numerous younger brothers, told me Tim had remarried in 1980.

I wouldn't have had a chance with him just then because he probably wasn't ready to divorce her yet, regardless of his feelings for me.

Being unattached for more than a few weeks was a new experience for me. I adjusted by spending more time reading. Or rather, I spent more time browsing the local independent bookstore, the one with comfortable chairs and loveseats sprinkled among the shelves. I spent many an afternoon reading books and meeting new men. On good days, I sipped beverages and conversed with new prospects in its small café.

One Saturday afternoon that fall—the best time to find unencumbered, intelligent men who weren't sports addicts—I picked a copy of Ken Follett's latest novel, *The Man from St. Petersburg,* and sauntered to my favorite reading area.

The store was surprisingly busy, so I took the only available seat on a tan leather couch, conveniently next to a handsome man who appeared to be the right age. I lowered myself carefully so as not to disturb him when I sat down and, when seated, fought my urges to stare. I wouldn't be able to get a good look sitting next to him anyway. I took in as much as I could without being obvious—a bit taller than me sitting down, medium build, salt and pepper hair, wire frame glasses.

Reading *Crime and Punishment* told me he was intelligent. Anybody reading Dostoevsky must be. He was dressed nicely in cords and an oxford shirt that looked like it was downgraded from office wear but was soft and comfortable. By leaning forward, I could see his penny loafers and smelled a hint of English Leather, very preppy. Starting a discussion about what he was reading would make me look like an idiot. I struggled to devise a not-too-obvious opening.

Clap. He snapped his book closed.

I winced.

"I'm sorry." He looked me in the eyes—his were cornflower blue, much like Tim's. "As much as I try, I get frustrated with this book. I've started it several times."

"I've never had the courage." *That sure was a weak way of introducing myself.*

"I'm taking a coffee break. Like to join me? I'll buy. It's the least I can do for being a bad neighbor." He stood and offered his hand to help me up.

"Okay." *There must be a God.* I kept holding his hand long after it was necessary because it felt so nice. He didn't seem to mind, and we walked hand in hand to the café area.

"I'm not usually that rude. Please believe me."

"I do. Are you an author?" *Could he be a tormented novelist with writer's block?*

"Yes, but not the kind you think."

"But you do write?" He had me confused.

"It depends on what you mean by write. If you're asking if I put words on blank pieces of paper, you're correct." He averted his eyes as if he was uncomfortable talking about this subject.

"What kind of words do you write?" I wondered if he wrote hard-core porn and was ashamed to tell me.

"Computerese and acronyms mostly. I'm a tech writer for a software company."

It wasn't exciting work, but it paid decently. Our two salaries could support a family.

He continued without making eye contact, "I'm almost embarrassed to say this, but I do like it."

"Since when is liking your job something to be ashamed of?" I most definitely didn't want someone who was about to quit his job and fly off to Tahiti to write the next great novel.

"My wife wanted me to make big money or be famous for writing best sellers. I can do neither."

No tan line on his ring finger. "I assume she's now the ex-Mrs...."

He nodded affirmatively. "Daniels, Nathaniel Daniels. My mother liked rhymes. Call me Nathan or Nate."

"I like it. It sounds so literary."

"What's your name?"

"Everybody calls me Tookie whether I like it or not, sort of like Cher, just one name."

We made introductory small talk for several minutes, continuing after we emptied our drinks. At a lull in the conversation, he looked out the window, then at his watch. A few seconds later, he started to get up.

"Tookie, I'm heading over to the state park to rent a canoe. It's the last day of their season, and I don't want to miss it. It's been nice meeting you."

"Good luck with *Crime and Punishment.*" *Damn. I thought for sure he'd ask for my number.*

He took three steps toward the door, stopped, and turned to me. "Like to come along?"

My mental telepathy worked. "Let me see your driver's license. A girl can't be too careful these days, what with the 'Thrill Killer' on the loose."

"Oh." He smiled as if he didn't know if I was serious or just kidding, but handed me his license.

His age was fine, his home address wasn't too far away, no DUI restrictions, and he was who he said he was. Evelyn had been with a guy who said he was a CIA agent but, when she showed me his photo, I recognized him from Carver-Watkins, where I worked for a decade after high school. Not only wasn't he a CIA agent, he was married.

"I'll follow you." I always drove myself separately, if possible, when getting picked up. It seemed safer. Plus, the assortment of clothing and gear stored in my trunk allowed me to join in on most any activity at a moment's notice. By buying cheap slacks and wearing comfortable shoes, I didn't worry about getting wet or staining my clothes canoeing.

Easy to follow, Nathaniel drove his Honda sedan at a moderate speed, signaling well ahead of turns. I'd been to the park numerous times and was familiar with the road. He drove directly to the canoe rental place. I put on my green head scarf and tortoiseshell sunglasses while he rented the canoe. Wearing these accessories made me feel more mysterious.

He couldn't have found a more romantic setting. The yellow sun reflected off the green-blue water, the rays creating sparkles along its path. Fall colors in hardwood's leaves contrasted the evergreens, as did my red hair against the scarf. Nathaniel, in his fringed suede jacket, reminded me of Daniel Day Lewis as Hawkeye paddling his canoe to rescue Cora from the deceitful Magua. Instead of interrogating him to learn the necessary information, I relaxed and let the romantic mood engulf me. We—the rhetorical we, as Nathaniel did most of the work— paddled to the farthest part of the lake and back along the shore. I had to help paddle to get back to the rental stand before closing time. My teeth chattered when the air cooled abruptly as the sun set.

He smiled. "Let's go to the lodge and have hot chocolate to warm up."

"Perfect." He couldn't know it, but the lodge was one of my favorite places.

ⲉⲟⲉⲟ

The hand-hewn log walls, stone fireplace, and random-width heart pine floors with Navajo rugs near the seating areas made this place the most romantic place in town. We drank hot chocolate at a cozy table near the fireplace. I fantasized Nathaniel in a Mountie uniform warbling, "I am calling you-ou-ou-ou-ou," to me. I wanted this afternoon to last forever. I was in love—and this time it was for real. By the time we left, the temperature had dropped even more, and my teeth chattered nonstop.

Nathaniel took off his jacket and put it over my shoulders as we walked to my car. "Better keep it for the drive home. It'll take your car quite a while to heat up."

"I promise to get it back to you." I put on a demure expression, not wanting to look too eager.

He held me around the waist. "I want to see you again."

"You will—tomorrow." Not wanting him to know he could have had me on the spot if he tried, I gently removed his hands and started to walk to my car. Realizing I was about to make a major mistake, I stopped. "Oh wait, I need your address."

He gave it to me, and I fantasized all night about what it would be like with him.

🙰🙰🙰

The next afternoon, I drove to his house wearing his jacket. He fiddled with a red Raleigh ten-speed bicycle in the driveway. "Want to go for a ride?"

"I didn't think to bring my bike."

"No problem. You can use Nate Jr.'s." He pointed to a black boys' Schwinn in the garage.

Having a son meant he must have some relationship skills and was, in the past, fertile.

At least the bike didn't have those awful dropped handlebars. "I've always ridden girls' bikes. I don't know if I can get on and off it." I wanted to be with Nathaniel, but I didn't want to look like a klutz.

"He's tall, but his bike has a small frame. I'll lower the seat for you."

He looked at the bike and back at my legs, then adjusted the seat. "Hop on."

I tried to lift my right leg over the top bar, but couldn't get it high enough.

"Watch me. Get on it like a cowboy mounts his horse." He put his left foot on his left pedal, coasted down the driveway, lifted his right leg over the back tire, swung it around, and landed his butt on the seat. I mimicked him and got on—awkwardly, but I was riding a boys' bike. I rode well enough to spend the afternoon with Nathaniel.

When we returned to his house, he had to help me off. It felt nice being in his arms, so I gave him his first kiss. We had supper at a casual, trendy place with a great salad bar near his house. I felt more relaxed with him than I had with anyone other than Tim. Conversation came easily, and neither of us was uncomfortable with silent stretches.

"I'd like to see you again, but I have the boys next weekend—every other weekend during the school year—so that's out. How about the weekend after that?"

Oh no. Not another Milt situation. "I'm allowed to go out on school nights now."

He laughed and blushed. "Of course. *Diner* is playing at the Bijou. I missed it when it first came out and hear it's really good."

"Wednesday it is. We can meet at the café down the block from it after work and get something to eat before the seven o'clock screening." Sometimes a girl had to help guys along. The trick was not looking too easy, especially when I really wanted a guy as much as I wanted Nathaniel. Being easy got me a lot of sex I wouldn't have otherwise had when I was younger, but snagging a father for my child required a different approach. And much more patience, something that was in short supply in my genes, and my jeans for that matter.

❧❧❧

I had let the romantic setting distract me from gathering intelligence on our canoe date but wouldn't let him escape without sharing the crucial information at dinner before the movie.

"Tell me about your boys."

His face lit up. "They're the joy of my life. I miss them terribly when Eloise has them."

"What happened to her?" Why did she let such a gem get away?

He slumped in his chair. "We lived fine on what I made, but she wanted more. She wanted me to apply for a job in Saudi Arabia, but I refused."

"Why'd she want to go to Saudi Arabia?" I couldn't imagine living in one of those countries with the way they treated women.

"She didn't. She wanted *me* to go and send back oodles of money."

"I don't understand."

"Her father was in the navy. He was out to sea most of the time. Her mother ran everything. When her father was in port, it was a big holiday until he shipped out again."

"Let me guess. Every day wasn't a holiday with you?"

"Bingo!" His face reflected his sadness.

"Why didn't you take her with you?"

"Families aren't allowed, just the workers. I would've been away from my boys for years."

"Years?" I couldn't imagine sending my husband off like that. She must not have loved him very much.

"Oh, yeah. Eloise wanted a lot more than one year's salary."

"So, she divorced you. Does she work?"

"She has a pretty good job with a fashion magazine. A benefit of that job is getting heavy discounts on clothing when she can't get them for free."

"Why'd you marry the clothes horse?"

"Everyone said she was perfect for me. We had similar backgrounds. Our parents were friends, and our friends were getting married. It was good when the first two boys were young. Mothering them kept her busy. She seemed to enjoy being a mom, but that changed when the third one came along."

"Didn't she want him?" She could have just had an abortion without telling Nathaniel.

"That pregnancy was a surprise. She wanted to abort him, but her parents would have disinherited her."

"What kept you with her so long?"

"I know this'll sound trite, but it was for the boys. That's not true—It was for me. I didn't want to give up my precious time with my sons."

"How long did that last?" He must have gone through a lot of agony. I would treat him a lot better than she ever did.

"Seeing her strategy fail, she threw me out of the house and filed for divorce."

Having heard what I needed to know, I looked at my watch. "It's time for our movie."

❧❧

I really enjoyed *Diner,* but had to refrain from laughing too hard at the popcorn scene. No guy ever pulled that one on me. Darn. I would have enjoyed finding his in the popcorn, but I kept my hands to myself like a good girl. Nathaniel seemed to enjoy being with me. He walked me to my car where I kissed him goodnight.

"I had a nice time and would like to see you again," I said, hoping he wouldn't think I was too forward.

Romance is highly underrated. When I was younger, I had little time for it because I thought it reduced my sex time. I was a fool. Now that I was looking for someone to father my daughter, romance became important because it cements relationships. I damned well didn't want to be divorced like so many of my boyfriends. Nathaniel was a romantic by nature, and I was in that kind of phase. We matched perfectly. Our relationship flourished, but I rationed sex—for me, not him. This time, it played a lesser role than usual because a child needs her father to enjoy being with her mother out of bed, not just in it.

Nathaniel's weekends with his sons provided me a block of uninterrupted time for planning future dates designed to establish a strong bond between us. Some of our "dates" consisted of working together on mundane tasks such as painting kids' bedrooms and moving me to an apartment closer to my new job and to him. We enjoyed each other's company even more as a result of working together.

Heavy winter snows arrived at the time we'd planned to introduce me to the boys. Thursday evening, I helped Nathaniel shovel his sidewalk.

"I'm not sure how we should go about doing this." Nathaniel looked troubled.

"Don't you just push the shovel under it, pick it up, and throw it aside?"

"I was talking about you meeting the boys."

"What's the big deal? Kids usually like me."

Looking very concerned, he said, "A year before we met, I introduced a woman I'd been seeing to them, and it was a disaster."

"What went wrong?" *His ex might be vindictive like Milt's.*

"The boys guard their time with me jealously. They viewed her as a competitor."

I put on my perkiest face. "We'll just have to try a different approach."

∽∾∽

On the next Saturday that had snow on the ground, I put my old sled in my trunk after breaking its ancient, frayed pull rope and met them at the slope nearest their house. Seeing Nathaniel's car, I parked where I'd have to go past it to get to the base of the hill. I passed the oldest boy, Nate Jr., as a stranger with an obvious problem, struggling to pull my sled up the hill against its will.

"It looks like you've got a problem," Nate Jr. said. "Can I help?"

"The rope broke." I showed it to him.

He looked it over and said, "Wait here."

The apple didn't fall far from the tree. He scampered back to their car, returning with a length of rope he had pulled out of the trunk. He replaced the rotted, broken rope in a jiffy. Soon, we were up at the top, where Nathaniel, Luke, and Josh wandered over to see what was up.

"I'm so grateful for your help," I gushed, "Thank you, so much! You're pretty kind for a teenager."

He puffed out his chest. "I'm Nate. I'm the oldest. I'm twelve, and these are my brothers. Luke's ten and Josh's eight. Oh, and this is my dad."

"It's nice to meet you Mr...." I feigned ignorance.

"Just call me Nathan. And you are..." He kept a straight face.

"Just call me Tookie."

"Would you like to ride down on our toboggan?" The ever-chivalrous Nate Jr. seemed to like me.

"I'd be honored." Phase one was accomplished.

ⅇ৩ⅇ৩

We all enjoyed ourselves immensely, but within an hour, the boys were chilled.

"Dad, let's go home," clacked little Josh through chattering teeth.

Nate Jr. whispered something to his father.

"Tookie, the boys and I'll be most honored if you'd share some hot chocolate with us at our humble abode."

"It is *I* who'd be honored to share a table with four such handsome men. But I must contribute something. Let's see if I have anything worthy of this event in my car. Who'll help me look?"

All three boys jumped at the chance and walked me to my car a short distance from theirs. I opened the passenger door and poked my hand into a grocery bag sitting on the seat.

"What do we have here?" I pulled the first item out of the bag.

"Bananas," said Luke.

"Graham crackers." Josh grinned.

"Orange juice." I held up the bottle for all to see, extending the suspense. No response.

"Marshmallows." Luke's eyes got wider.

"Cranberry juice." I waved the bottle to no reaction.

I pulled the last item out slowly, hiding it from view until I was ready for them to see it. "Any one like Hershey bars?" I wagged them in their faces.

"S'mores," shouted all three boys simultaneously.

"I should ride with you so you don't get lost," offered Nate Jr.

"Is that all right with you, Nathan? Your son is so chivalrous. Is his father?"

"Sometimes." Nathaniel's eyes twinkled. "You may

ride with her, Nate. Be sure to buckle your seatbelt."

"Can we go, too?" asked the other two.

"There's room if someone holds the groceries on his lap." I held the bag up for them to see.

"Hand it to me," said Nate Jr. as he buckled himself into the passenger seat.

Phase two was complete.

Nathaniel led the way at a slower than normal speed on the snow-packed road. Nate Jr. gave me explicit directions as if I couldn't see where his father's car was going.

Arriving at his house, we all raced into their roomy but spare kitchen, that lacked a woman's touch, to get out of the cold. The boys supervised Nathaniel closely as he prepared the hot chocolate. I got out of their way and started a fire in the fireplace while waiting in the inviting family room. *Floral drapes would brighten this room wonderfully.*

"Come and get it." Nathaniel ladled copious quantities of hot chocolate into our cups, then Josh plopped a marshmallow into each. We retired to the hearth where I took charge of making the S'mores. It reminded me of when I took care of my younger brothers. They loved S'mores as much as Mike and Jack had.

I excused myself to go to the bathroom when the boys started round-two on their own. On the way back, I eavesdropped from the hallway.

"Dad," Nate Jr. started, "Luke, Josh, and I've been thinking about this for a while. It's time you started dating. Tookie's not glamorous like Mom, but she's lots of fun. Whadya think, Dad?"

Phase three was successful.

"I think you're jumping the gun. What makes you think she'd consider going out with me?"

"She came here, didn't she?" countered Josh.

"I've got to admit she's brave consorting with the likes of us. Did it ever occur to you that she was freezing and only came in here to get in out of the cold?"

"She didn't have to share her S'mores with us. Ask her to stay for dinner. We could send out for pizza. If she stays, it'd be a pretty good sign she likes being with us," said Nate Jr.

"I can't argue with your logic."

I fiddled with my compact as I walked back into the family room, trying to look unaware of what'd just transpired.

"Tookie, Dad wants to ask you something," said Nate Jr.

"I know we're a pretty motley crew, but will you stay and have dinner with us? It'll only be pizza?" Nathaniel avoided looking directly at me to keep a straight face.

"It depends on what kind you order," I teased.

"We're getting two large vegetarian pizzas with pepperoni," announced Luke.

"Isn't that a lot of pizza?" *One's enough for four girls.*

"You haven't been around growing boys for a while, have you?" said Nathaniel.

I held my arms out wide. "I'm yours for the evening."

After we put the boys to bed, we cuddled by the fireplace. The entire afternoon and evening were one big "Kodak moment" for me. I yearned to be a mom so badly, and I loved playing one that day. Before going to bed, the boys insisted I spend the next visitation Saturday with them. It was like a dream come true, with only one exception: I wanted a daughter of my own and had for a long, long time. Phase four was successful.

That night elevated our relationship a step, but Nathaniel acted skittish whenever the topic of marriage was raised. His wife had hurt him deeply. It'd be a long time before he could trust a woman enough to marry again.

∽∾∽∾

When spring broke, I flew out to Memphis to visit my parents across the Mississippi in Arkansas. My brother, Daniel, lived with them and looked after them in their old age instead of getting a job. It gave him lots of time to play chess, the only thing he enjoyed doing.

He picked me up at the airport.

Seeing Daniel was alone, I asked, "Where's Dad?"

Deadpan, he said, "He didn't make it."

"Why not? I talked to him this morning just before leaving for the airport. He said he'd meet me."

"He didn't make it." Daniel put his hands on his hips and looked away from me.

"You mean—"

"He's dead. It wasn't a heart attack. They said it was a blood clot in his lung."

This can't be true. I raced to the restroom, but didn't

make it, and threw up all over the floor.

Daniel had the car radio tuned to a station that broadcast local news from the small towns in the area. Hearing my father's obituary on the radio was surreal. I'd never heard of such a thing before and hadn't yet accepted that he was really gone. No longer having a father left a huge hole in my life. Missing him didn't stop. I was his favorite. He burst into the house grinning after work, and we'd huddle around him. No man enjoyed being a father more.

I wasn't ready for what I'd encounter when we arrived at their home. Dad retired early after getting out of the hospital from a nervous breakdown caused by the company's threat to computerize his office. A little frame house near Mom's parents in Arkansas was all they could afford on their meager savings and small pension.

Daniel reacted strangely. He didn't shed a tear. He set about removing every trace of Dad from the house without emotion. I couldn't believe he was doing that. Dad couldn't be dead. It wasn't fair. I'd never get to see him again. Did he have to throw out Dad's Mentos? I knew no one else liked them and wouldn't eat them, but Dad always had them around.

It might have been a relief for Mother after decades of constant worrying about his heart giving out. She didn't cry. She just said, "I'm so sorry for you, Mary Louise." I wondered if she would be happier and stop drinking.

I never heard a cross word between my parents. My father idolized my mother and wouldn't have survived if she'd gone first. Now, she could go on without him. Time would tell if it was for better or worse.

What had started out as a long weekend visit with my parents was weirdly extended to include his funeral. My siblings, who could, made it in. The house seemed so strange with no evidence of Dad ever having been there, and Mother serenely dealing with everything a widow must deal with on the death of her husband. I halfway expected her to break into tears in the church or, for sure, at his grave. But she didn't. She remained stoic through the whole thing. I now doubt that she ever shed a tear. Mike and Jack, being the youngest, took his death harder than Beth and Daniel. The five of us wouldn't be together again until Mom died much later.

Losing Dad made it all the more clear to me how precious is the time we have on this earth to do those things we want to do. It was time to move my relationship with Nathaniel forward.

❧❧❧

He picked me up at the airport when I returned home and drove me to my apartment.

"Come in for a while? I need to talk." I couldn't wait any longer. I took Nathaniel's hand and walked him toward the couch. I stopped halfway and reached for his other hand. Holding both of them, I said, "I know this isn't Leap Year or anything." I drew in a deep breath and looked him straight in the eyes. "But I'm going to do this anyway, Nathan. Will you marry me?"

The color fell from his face, and his hands turned cold.

"Before you answer—I want a child. Two if the first isn't a girl." I closed my eyes and held my breath. I was still holding his hands.

"I can't do that, Tookie. I love you very much. I'd marry you in an instant, but I don't want any more children."

I opened my eyes, let out my breath, and dropped his hands. I felt my life slipping away from me. My father's death brought that into clear focus. I'd wanted a daughter for as long as I could remember. I felt a huge void inside me whenever I saw a little girl with her mother. I'd soon be thirty-three and couldn't wait much longer. The older a woman is, the harder it is to get pregnant, and the higher the likelihood of birth defects. I had to get serious about this right now.

"We'll talk." He gently placed his hands on my shoulders and kissed me on the forehead. Then he turned slowly, walked across the room and out the door.

We never talked. He wanted no more children and, frankly, couldn't afford them. To me, marriage without children made no sense. After a time, Nathaniel and I established a pattern of having dinner once a month as friends. The romance was over for me when he refused to give me a child.

☙❧

I dated around feverishly for about a year, but none

of the men I met were husband material, or at least not husband material for me. To increase my chances of finding someone, I told everyone I knew I wanted to get married and start a family. They fixed me up with numerous blind dates, all of which turned out to be duds.

The podiatrist found my arches to be perfect, but had no interest in any other part of my body. Playing a dominatrix wearing sexy black leather for the masochistic mayor of a little town on the way to my work was fun at first, but no way did I want my picture in the paper anywhere near his, even if it was innocent. I had high hopes when Harvey got me excited by telling me he wanted in my panties. But I was let down when he strutted around the room in them. Then came the dud I didn't allow myself to recognize as such.

CHAPTER 9

Blind Date

1984:

My clock ticked constantly and deafeningly. Few waking moments weren't spent looking for a husband or worrying if I'd ever find one. And the pool was most definitely shallow. Year by year, I found fewer and fewer men to date who were less than a decade older than me, and those who were available were of an ever-lowering quality.

Almost all the girls from my high school class were married, or at least had children, and I was alone like a well-used keyhole. I had been on so many disastrous fix-ups with strange men, one of whom was actually blind. He was so obnoxious, he wouldn't have had any friends if he had sight. Considerable restraint was required to keep from kneeing him in the balls when he made a crack about Jersey girls being dumb.

I wanted a daughter so badly, any single man, no

matter how undesirable, was a possibility. Thirty-four, childless, only proposed to once, and that when I was only eighteen, I briefly considered calling Tim. I hadn't heard he divorced, but he could have. His second was nearing the half-life of marriages, so it was possible he was available. But not wanting to explain myself if another angry wife answered the phone nixed that idea.

Sandy, a new girl at work, took me aside one day. "Don, my husband, and I would like you to come for dinner Friday."

This sounds kinky. "But your husband doesn't know me." *How could he want me in a ménage a trois?*

She smiled. "A guy he works with is unattached, and Don is an unrepentant matchmaker."

"A blind date? Tell me more about him."

"Oliver's about your age, taller than you, dark curly hair."

"What does he do?"

"He's an engineer. Makes more than Don." Her grin suggested that she wished Don made more.

Too perfect. "How many ex-wives and children?"

"None." She smiled as if no ex-wives and kids is a good thing for a thirty-four-year-old man.

"None?" *Never married. No kids. Can't commit to a relationship.*

"He still lives at home and wants to get out."

"What is he, a momma's boy?"

"His parents are "old country" from eastern Europe somewhere."

"Doesn't sound like much of a prize."

"I thought you were looking for fun, not a husband," She lifted her hands, palms up.

"I changed my mind. I want my daughter to have her father's name." *But this guy doesn't sound like Mr. Right. I turned to walk away.*

"Oh. His parents are hounding him for a grandson."

I stopped in my tracks. "What time Friday?" *My future in-laws just might put me on the baby train.*

❦

Friday night, mischievous Don sat at the head of their table for six, Sandy at the foot, Ollie slouched across from me. He looked better than advertised: almost six feet, dark complexion, handsome enough, and seemed to be intelligent whenever he spoke.

After introductions and small talk, I thought it best to get to the point of the event. "Have you always lived at home?"

"Always. I wanted to live in on campus at college, but my mother wouldn't hear of it."

"What was your major?" *Let's see how smart he is. If he was in art history or general studies, I'm bailing.*

"Physics. Yours?"

I settled in for the evening.

Don retrieved more beers from the kitchen. I declined his offer again. Ollie pushed his two empties back to make room for two fresh ones.

"Applied stats at State U. Your school?" *Let me guess. Small private school.*

"Chatham College, class of seventy-two, Alpha Sigma Sigma."

Even worse, he was a spoiled frat boy. At least he was smart—and his parents could afford to send him to Chatham.

"Tookie, do you want to help me clear?" asked Sandy, alternating between giving me the eye and glancing at the table.

"Sure." I picked up Don's and my dirty dishes and carried them into the kitchen.

Sandy followed me in with hers and Ollie's china and set about hand washing them. I squatted by the door to the dining room to peek and eavesdrop through the keyhole. I couldn't waste any more time. My eggs were speeding to their fertilize-by date. The men talked mostly about sports and cars. That neither brought up politics or religion was fine with me. I've little interest in them, either.

All too soon, they got around to me.

"Well, Ollie, what do you think of Tookie?" Don asked, looking Ollie over like a car salesman evaluated a prospective buyer.

"Ehh." He shrugged. "She's not as good looking as most girls I date."

He'll think I'm better looking after I suck the chrome off his trailer hitch. They always do.

"I have to admit she doesn't have much." Don gestured as if he was bouncing the rack I didn't have, looking disappointed and not wanting to disagree with a "customer."

"Nice ass for a woman her age." Ollie winked at Don and smiled.

He'll like me better in form-fitting slacks.

Seeing some interest, Don moved in to close the deal. "Sandy says she broke up with her last boyfriend months ago and hasn't dated anybody since then."

Ollie's eyes opened like saucers. "So, she's looking for some action?"

You're in my department now.

"I'd think so," smirked Don, nodding his head before taking another swig of beer.

"I'd have no problem giving her a little." Ollie grabbed the air with both hands, jerking them back as he thrust his hips forward like he was buggering me doggie style.

At least he's not gay.

I whispered to Sandy, "What did you say to Don about me?"

"Not much. He's an unashamed matchmaker and will say whatever it takes to get two people together, no matter how ill-suited."

I whispered as loudly as I dared, "Did you tell Don I'm horny and looking to get laid?"

She shushed me.

"I take that as a yes."

Guilty, Sandy lifted her shoulders, and I returned to my post at the keyhole.

"Why haven't you married, Ollie?" Don sounded sincere, having gotten hitched two years out of college.

"Why buy the cow when the milk's free? Whenever I

want it, I don't have to look very far. Single girls today don't want to be tied down, but still want to play hide the salami, and even more married women want something on the side." He looked self-satisfied.

You don't know what it's like to hide your salami in me. You'll come back for more.

"Don't you want a wife to share your life with?" Don looked sincere and nervous, as if he feared letting a fish escape his hook.

"Don't need one. My mother takes care of everything around the house, doesn't charge me much, and doesn't hassle me."

I'll see about that. Your mother won't do for you what I will.

As men's conversations often do, they turned to jokes and, with no women around, some were downright disgusting. I like dirty jokes as well as anyone, better than many men, in fact, but theirs were old and lame for the most part. And some of Ollie's were sexist.

"Question: What do you call a room full of women, half with PMS, half with yeast infections? Answer: A whine and cheese party."

Both laughed hysterically at Ollie's crude joke.

I figured he wasn't much different than most men in that regard. I'd work on that when we were married.

When Sandy finished with the dishes and my muscles ached from squatting, we returned to the dining room.

The four of us conversed for an hour, then Sandy yawned, her hint for us to leave. That also gave Ollie and me a little time to ourselves. We said our goodbyes to our hosts and shifted to the front porch.

We talked for a few minutes about nothing in particular. He was the perfect height, about four inches taller than me, with an athletic build and had all of his teeth that showed. I would swear I saw a hint of red in his hair. My baby must be a ginger. No green eyes, though. That was too much to hope for.

"Ollie, Sandy didn't give me your phone number." I fumbled through my purse for a pen and address book.

"Here's my card." He handed me his business card.

Seeing only his work number, I asked, "What's your home number?"

"Five, five, five, six, nine, eight, one."

After writing his number in my book, I said, "I don't have a card."

"Don't worry about it. I can look it up in the book."

That's not very encouraging.

He glanced at his watch. "Didn't realize it's so late. I've got an early tee-time tomorrow. Next Saturday?" And off he rushed.

"Okay?" *Not even a hug or a handshake. Nothing. But he did ask me out, sorta. Why am I always attracted to smart guys with no social skills?*

He hopped into his car and pulled away without looking back in my direction.

Hmm. Drives a Mercedes. Surely makes enough to support a family. We could trade it in for a four-door when the baby comes.

Seeing me left standing alone on the porch looking at

the stars, Sandy came out. "What do you think?"

"Our children will have red hair, don't you think?"

"Don't you think you should slow down a little?" She looked concerned, as if I was doing something stupid.

"Look, I was thirty-four on St. Swithin's Day and my clock ticks so loudly I have to use earplugs to get any sleep. I can't wait any longer."

"All I can tell you is to look before you leap." She drilled me with her eyes.

I looked away. "Has he slept with many women?"

"Probably, but he's never had a real relationship. Dinner and sex on Saturday night with a pretty girl, but nothing more than that."

"I wonder why he wants to go out with me?"

"Tookie! You *are* pretty. Besides that, his mother wants grandchildren."

"You're wrong. He thinks I'm easy. Don told him."

If Ollie's mother wanted grandchildren, this would be a match made in heaven—Ollie's mother and me. We had to become allies to get Ollie to do the right thing. I couldn't leave anything to chance.

એન્જ

I called him at work early the next week before he changed his mind or forgot about our date to lock him in for Saturday night.

"Hi, Ollie."

"Hello?"

He didn't recognize my voice. That's not a good sign. "It's Tookie. We need to make plans for Saturday night so I know how to prepare."

"Okay?" he said, without any enthusiasm.

"*Amadeus* will be at the Bijou Saturday. The reviews say it's great. Let's meet at the café down the block and grab a bite to eat before the show."

Ollie was used to taking orders from his mother. I'd shift that function to me quickly enough. It always looks good to meet a guy somewhere safe for the first date because it makes him think you're cautious and responsible. I picked *Amadeus* because Mozart was pretty randy, and Ollie would probably like that part of it, if nothing else. It was far too early in our relationship to drag him to a chick flick.

Ollie was punctual. That's one thing I demand from my men. I had a chicken salad. He had a Reuben. We chatted while we ate. I let him take the lead in the conversation to learn more about him.

"I graduated from St. Ignasius in 1968."

"Bayshore the same year," I said.

He chuckled. "Oh, no. We were school rivals."

"Really? I moved in from the Midwest during my senior year, and don't know anything about the rivalries."

"Have a roommate?" He seemed to listen more closely for my answer to this question than for any of the others.

Make him work to get the answer he wants to hear. "Yes."

"Always?"

"Until my sister married."

"So, you still live at home?" He sounded as if he was starting to get frustrated.

"Not since I was eighteen."

He frowned. "I meant now."

He's not very subtle. "No. My apartment's big enough, but I prefer my privacy."

"What about guests?"

"Depends on who it is." *And it isn't going to be you until I say so.*

"Overnight?"

"Does your mother allow that?" *Let's see how short a lease she has you on.*

"If I tell her I'm not coming home." He was unfazed.

"Are your parents well off?"

"They're frugal and save most of what Dad makes."

"Are you a saver, too?"

"Not like they are."

Grandma and Grandpa might be able to fund our kids' college.

After *Amadeus*, he wasn't ready to end our date and led me toward his car. I got him talking about himself and learned I'd have to cut back his golf, among other things, for family time. The money it cost would go toward paying our mortgage.

"The night's young. Let's pick up a six-pack and go to your place." He looked at me with lust in his heart, just what I wanted.

He was attractive, and I probably wanted it more than he did, but I couldn't let him think I was easy if I was going to pry him loose from his mother.

"Frankly, I'm tired after sitting for three hours. The movie was great, and I thank you for taking me to it. Let's just talk in your car for a few minutes while we arrange our next date." Using the assumptive close sales technique worked on men. They got locked into dates because they hadn't had to learn how to say no and didn't want to look like ogres. They preferred to just not call you again to avoid uncomfortable conversations. I didn't let them off that easy if I was interested.

He unlocked the driver's door, then, from the inside, unlocked mine so I could get in.

More bad manners for my list of things I'd have to correct. I centered myself in the passenger seat, close enough for him to kiss me but far enough to get away in case he got grabby.

"Please don't take my being tired as a reflection of this date. I had a good time and want to see you again." Directness like this disarmed men and put them on their heels. While he gathered his thoughts, I retrieved my Parker Brothers fountain pen from my purse and palmed it. As he reached over to kiss me, I stopped him by firmly pressing my other hand against his chest.

"Not yet. We haven't arranged our next date."

Once I had him locked in for the next weekend, I didn't just let him kiss me goodnight, I gave him a real smoocheroo. If he only wanted me half as much as I wanted him, he'd see me again as soon as he could.

While he was kissing me, I dropped my pen where he wouldn't see it. The way to some men's hearts was through their stomachs, for others it was through their baby makers. For Ollie, I was sure it was through his mother. Operation Dropped Pen would introduce me to her.

✦✦✦

The next afternoon, Sunday, around three, I called his house.

"Ahoj," answered someone who sounded like she wasn't expecting a call.

"This is Tookie, the girl Oliver took to the movies last night."

"Vat can I do for you?" She sounded cool and distant in the voice of an older woman with an eastern European accent.

"Could you please give me directions to your house. My expensive fountain pen fell out of my purse in his car last night."

She gave me precise directions without consulting Ollie. My assumption that his controlling mother would want to look me over was correct. The way to a ring on the third finger of my left hand was through his mother. I was sure of that.

✦✦✦

Fortunately, it was an easy fifteen-minute drive from my apartment. Ollie would find me conveniently located. I quickly found the address. He lived in a meticulously maintained, modest white-frame home. I parked in the driveway and walked to the closest door and pressed the button firmly but not long enough to be annoying.

A plump older woman opened the inside door and looked out at me through the glass storm door. Her sour look turned to one of curiosity as she took a few seconds to look me over.

"I'm so sorry to bother you, it being Sunday and all." I tried to be as nonthreatening as possible.

"Are you Oliver's girlfriend?"

Better call him Oliver in front of her. I nodded, inaudibly saying, "I hope so."

"It's not a bodder," she said and pushed the door open. "Come right in, Tookie."

The butterflies in my stomach settled a bit after receiving a warm reception.

"Thank you." I walked into an old people's living room cluttered with photos and knickknacks, sparkling clean down to the plastic slipcovers on the upholstered furniture.

"Vat gorgeous red hair you have, Tookie."

"Thanks. I noticed a bit or red in Oliver's hair. Does it run in your family?" *That'd be a plus.*

"Not like yours—which is beautiful—but a hint of it on both sides. Bert!"

On the far side of the room, I saw Bert sitting in his easy chair reading the Sunday paper. They must have been nearly forty when they had Ollie, because they looked more like grandparents.

"Vat do you vant, Rose?" He said in a less pronounced accent and had the look of a man who didn't like being disturbed.

At least their accents weren't so bad I couldn't understand them. I wondered where they were from. Hungary maybe.

"Father, I need you to find dis young lady's pen in Oliver's car," she said with a sweetness that didn't seem to fit her.

"Can't he do dat himself?" Bert looked irritated.

"No need to bodder him now. I'd like to get to know his girlfriend a little better. Let's go look for it."

Girlfriend! She must like me.

Bert guided us out to the car. He wasn't nearly as tall as Ollie, but it was clear where Ollie's looks and curly hair came from. His mother, who followed us, was much shorter and plumper. She apparently liked to cook, or eat anyway. Both parents were very gray, way too gray to determine if theirs had ever been red. Rose followed us out to the car. Once, when I turned, I saw her eyeing up my ass. While Bert searched in Ollie's car for my pen, she positioned herself to look me up and down from the front.

Was she some sort of pervert?

After a few minutes reaching under the passenger seat, Bert saw that the pen had rolled to the floor of the back seat. "Is dis it? It's a very nice vun." He looked pleased with himself, probably more that he had found it than wasting time with a stranger.

"Yes. Thank you. This pen's very dear to me. My grandmother gave it to me when I graduated. I was the first one in my family to go to college." I proudly lied about the pen but not my achievement.

"Oliver was the first in ours." It was easy to see Rose was proud of that.

"I really appreciate you finding it for me."

"You can dank us by eating wid us tonight. Ve don't have many pretty young girls as guests, and ve eat early on Sundays."

"I really shouldn't impose."

"Oliver's cookink tonight. He likes Italian. Do you?"

"I love it. I wouldn't miss this for the world." *I'm in. Now to find out how far.*

Once we were back in the living room, I noticed Ollie's baby picture on an old but dustfree table with other family photographs. It was hard to believe at first, but Rose was very pretty when she was young. She looked like a tart in her flapper dress. A tiny Czechoslovakian flag was taped onto a photo of what must've been Ollie's grandparents.

"May I use the restroom?"

She pointed down the short hall. "It's the second door on the left."

I didn't have to pee, but I needed to be out of the room for them to speak freely. Like many older people with less than perfect hearing, Ollie's parents spoke loudly to hear each other.

The thin wood panel on the bathroom door amplified the sound and made it easy for me to take in everything without eavesdropping.

"Why on earth did you invite dat girl to dinner? Ve

hardly know her, and you didn't even tell Oliver she's here."

"Did you see her pánevní?" said Rose. "She's *plodný*, a baby-makink machine. Tookie vill give us our grandson."

"She has no cecky. How vill she nurse him?"

"Her *prsa* vill fill vid milk ven she gets pregnant. Ven her cecky develop, our grandson is on his vay."

"I'll watch for that." His voice sounded less grumpy.

"Zvrhlík!" She chuckled.

Having heard all I needed to hear, I flushed the toilet for cover and floated back to the living room.

"Sit, sit, please." She pointed to a chair opposite her. "Tell me about yourself. Ve should know each other better, yes? My Oliver, he has told us so little of you. Such a beautiful voman. Such a lucky man is my son."

What a nice feeling it was to have a guy's mother like me for a change.

I told them the truth. "I'm Oliver's age and work as a statistician at a major pharmaceutical company."

"Ever been married?" She got friendlier with each question.

"No."

"Engaged?"

"Not even close." *So far so good and no need to lie.*

"Why not?" She frowned. Maybe she thought something was wrong with me.

"Men don't want families these days." I lied only about Tim.

"You like children, don't you?"

"I love children and want some of my own. I practically raised my two youngest brothers." I was on a truth roll. That hadn't happened since I dated Tim.

"You have little time to vaste."

"Unfortunately, it takes a man, too, and the right one hasn't come along yet," I said with more unfortunate accuracy.

"Maybe he has. Let's take a look in the kitchen."

CHAPTER 10

Ollie

S omething smells good," I said to keep the discussion with Rose and Bert going as we waited in their living room. The sound of pots and pans clanging interrupted our conversation.

"Oliver," trilled Rose, as she poked her head into the kitchen, "Dere vill be four for supper."

"What?" answered Ollie loudly enough for us to hear in the living room. He burst through the swinging door. Seeing me, he stopped dead in his tracks, looking completely perplexed.

I couldn't tell if he was pleased to see me or thought I was stalking him.

Before he had a chance to say something she didn't like, Rose jumped in, "Your girlfriend has agreed to eat vid us tonight. Isn't it nice to have a young lady in de house?"

Better give him my excuse. "My pen must have fallen out of my purse when we were talking last night." I pulled it out and waved it for Ollie to see. *Is that a tiny smile?*

"Okay, I'll make sure there's enough." He retreated to the kitchen, still looking confused as to how I had outmaneuvered him.

That Ollie liked to cook was an unexpected bonus. Whether he was good at it would be answered shortly. The broken fountain pen I'd found had come in handy several times, but none produced results to compare with this.

I helped Rose with the dishes and thought it best to leave when we were finished. And yes, the linguini with Alfredo sauce and white wine was delicious. Lucky me.

On the way to my car, Ollie said, "My parents really enjoyed having you over tonight, Tookie." When he put his arm around my waist in preparation for a goodnight kiss, I clasped my hands around his neck to pull his head down to my mine and kissed him passionately, with the tiniest bit of tongue at the end. Afterward, I remained silent, putting the pressure on him to say something.

"I have tickets for the Rutgers game Saturday."

Football, smootball, what did I care? He was planning dates now. Things were moving faster than I hoped. "What time are you picking me up?"

"Ten. It's an early game."

Whoa! He thinks he's gonna pork me beforehand. "They play football in the morning?"

"No. I tailgate with frat brothers a couple hours before the game. It's a ritual." He looked at me as if I was from Mars because, although I went to college, I knew nothing about undergrad or alumni social life.

Totally befuddled at this point, I asked, "What should I bring?"

"Cranberry juice. They'll have tons of food and beer, but nothing you'll drink."

I nodded. "Bye."

He walked me to my car where I gave him a peck on the lips before getting behind the wheel.

"Hey," he shouted with a shit-eating grin, "Bring your pom-poms, too."

I had to stop myself from giving him the finger. He should have known I was sensitive about my tiny breasts.

⋘⋙

My gynecologist was out of the country and couldn't see me immediately. After getting pregnant using an IUD before, I wasn't confident in anyone other than her removing it.

I had been buying sponges by the gross and popping them in before dates to be doubly protected. So, I had to hold Ollie off a while longer. I didn't dare get naked with him with the incriminating string dangling out of me. Ollie would consider me his personal playground and demand I keep the IUD. Unable to fake having one in place, I could only hide sponges in strategic places in my apartment where they would be most handy when needed.

⋘⋙

Ollie introduced me to his friends and their wives at the tailgate before the game. They had married pretty sorority girls. I could tell by how they dressed, styled their hair, and wore their makeup. In other words, they had little in common with me. However, I'd worked myself up to a better job than many of them had. But most of them were staying home with their kids then. I was jealous. I wanted a baby so badly, I needed Ollie to want one, too. A boy might even be better than nothing.

Beer flowed freely. Tongues and propriety loosened after the cans from the first case stood like dead soldiers sacrificed to the cause. Their calling each other by nicknames made keeping them straight impossible. Jungle—I think that was the animal's name—leered at me much of the afternoon. After several beers, he stumbled over.

"Is what they say about redheads with freckles true?" he slurred.

"I don't know." I glared at him over the top of my cranberry juice mug. "What do they say?"

"They say redheads with freckles enjoy sex more than any other women." He winked.

"You'll never know." I turned my back to the slob.

A couple of the guys snickered after hearing my retort.

I walked over to the table to get more potato salad.

"Does Oliver?" asked another of his fraternity brothers as he staggered to the cooler to retrieve another beer.

I felt cheap being thought of as nothing more than his current nookie.

Ollie stepped in, "You're out of line, Goober. No more beer for you."

At least he played the gallant this time.

The pageantry of the game on a fall afternoon was spectacular in itself. The colors of the band, the teams, and the fans added to the fall foliage outside the stadium, making it a truly striking scene. I didn't keep track of the score and didn't even know or care who was playing. Not being very coordinated, I never cared much for sports.

I had watched football on Sunday afternoons with Dad and Tim several times. The best part was sitting next to him and feeling the side of his body pressed against mine without my parents noticing.

I also got to listen to Dad's running commentary, which was quite entertaining. I do remember Mom was a Cowboys fan, and Dad cheered for Johnny Unitas and the Colts, but I never had any idea why either of them liked those teams.

Waiting stalled in the traffic jam exiting the parking lot after the game gave us time to talk.

Before I could think of something safe to say, Ollie asked, "Where'd you like to go for dinner?"

Perfect. "I feel tired and grungy. Would it be all right to pick up Chinese and eat it at my place?"

I think I saw a twinkle in his eye. "Okay by me."

On arriving at my apartment, I baited him some more. "Ollie, could you set the table and put our food on plates, please? I need a quick shower."

He looked me up and down as if he was hungry for some American rather than Chinese. "No problem. I can always nuke our plates if they're not warm enough when you're done."

I came back refreshed wearing lounging pajamas to find the drapes closed and Barry White playing on my stereo. Ollie had taken off his shoes.

"I just had to get into something soft and comfortable." Over my most opaque panties.

"I like how you look in them." His smile told me he expected to see me with even less on in a few short minutes.

"Let's eat off the coffee table?" I asked in my sexiest, softest voice. "It's too stuffy to eat Chinese in the dining room."

Ollie almost broke a leg moving our plates and drinks to the living room. "How's this?"

I sat close to him, on his left in an ideal make-out position and took a forkful of moo goo gai pan. "Much better. Like some of mine?" I turned to look into Ollie's eyes as I put a forkful in his mouth.

"Thanks, this is good. Try mine." His look told me he had something more than Cantonese cuisine on the brain.

We must not have been terribly hungry as our quarter-eaten plates were quickly set aside, and we were necking up a storm. I wore no bra to give Ollie free access. In case he had any doubts where I wanted his attention, I left the top two buttons open as a hint. If he didn't know we small breasted women enjoy being fondled more than our better-endowed sisters, he sure faked it well.

I said, "You're not finished here," whenever he tried

to move lower before I was ready. I'd move his hand or mouth, whichever I wanted at that time, to Lucy or Ethel, the one most needing attention. Eventually, he got the hint. He molested my titties so thoroughly I drenched the panties that hid the incriminating string.

"Mmmmuh." I panted and moaned, while involuntarily arching my back.

Ollie went for my crotch again.

I grasped his wrist firmly and pulled it aside. "I'm not ready yet."

"You're hot enough to grill steaks."

"Damn right I want it. But we hardly know each other."

Ollie froze like a spoiled kid who wasn't getting what he wanted.

"Don't pout," I hadn't expected to get this excited so soon, so I had to forge a new plan out of necessity.

"You're not going to leave me like this?" He looked down at the large bulge in his slacks.

"Of course not. I'm no prick teaser." I stood up. "Give Little Ollie some air."

He stood and dropped his pants and drawers.

I retrieved a bottle of Cornhuskers' Lotion and a pair of yellow rubber gloves from under the sink and sat on the couch. Patting the place next to me, I said, "Sit down."

Ollie tried to pull my head down.

"No." I slapped his hand. "Relax, or you won't get anything." To make my point, I simulated the thumb and forefinger flick nurses employ to deflate aroused patients.

After he released me, I started to pull on my left glove with an exaggerated motion.

"You're not wearing those while you whack me off, are you?" He looked as if he couldn't believe what he was seeing.

"Isn't this how sorority girls do it?" I tried to sound serious.

He was irritated with me. "No! That was a joke in *Animal House*."

Some men didn't appreciate my sense of humor. Although not my favorite means of pleasuring a man, I was quite competent with my hands and put them to work. Ollie stopped resisting and relaxed as much as a man can when having his chicken choked. Assuming he hadn't had sex recently, I prolonged the stroking as long as possible to extend his desire to the maximum and his ultimate pleasure to the fullest.

Relieved, he collapsed onto the couch. "Thanks. I feel a lot better now. If it's all the same to you, I'd like to stay here tonight."

"Whoa! Way too soon for any of that." I jumped up and handed him his coat.

At the door, I said, "I really enjoyed the day with you, Ollie. All of it."

"Me, too, but I'm too tired to drive now."

"Next Saturday, I'd like to take in *La Cage Aux Folles* in the city. I hear it's very good."

"Isn't it about gay guys?" He looked uncomfortable.

"The reviews say it's very funny. Get the tickets." I wasn't sure he thought I was worth it.

He didn't look like he thought I was, as he said with a look of resignation, "I'll call you with the details."

He did.

ᘓᘔ

Overall, things were working out well. His friends seeing us as a couple was very important, much more so than my friends seeing us that way. I'd give them their chance later. It was too early in our relationship for mid-week dates, but sex wasn't too far off in the future.

From that point forward, his parents invited me for supper every Sunday. Rose wasn't about to let a potential grandchild-factory get away, and I'd make sure Ollie didn't let that happen. I made a point of being very proper and respectful. No sharp tongue. No sexual innuendos. No dirty jokes. No playing with Ollie under the table. Landing a husband exacted tremendous sacrifice.

After a month of becoming a fixture at Rose's Sunday suppers, she phoned me late one Sunday morning, saying only, "Ve need to talk. Come at two," then hung up.

She sounded serious, and I didn't want to cross her. So, I arrived two minutes early. Bert passed me going the opposite direction as I approached their driveway. Ollie's car was gone. I took a second after parking to collect myself before facing the unknown. Rose opened the door before I could knock and brusquely ushered me into the house.

Once in, she looked out the window to make sure we

were alone. "Sit your ass dere, you little kurva," she said in her Czech accent. She pointed to a chair in the living room and sat on the sofa directly across from me. "Vat do you have to say for yourself, Miss Carver-Vatkins Blow-job Queen of 1970?"

"Er…1971 to 1977," I said, unable to look at her, trying not to throw up.

"And you're proud of dat?" She sounded less than pleased with my response.

"Whenever I do something, I strive to do my best."

"Look at me ven I'm speakink to you," Rose said, clearly upset.

I raised my head but couldn't look at her.

Lifting my chin to look me straight in the eyes, she said, "I've lived in dis area all my adult life and know people, vun of whom is a private investigator who owes me favors."

Oh shit!

"You've got a history. One helluva history. You've been around—a lot. De investigator put it very crudely, but accurately. 'If she had as many peckers stickink out of her as she had poked into her, she'd look like a porcupine.'"

I felt sick to my stomach. "You want me to disappear?"

"Did you really sleep vith all de men at Carver-Vatkins?" She drew her eyebrows down, looking hawk-like.

"Not all of them," I answered with as much dignity as I could muster.

"I bet you didn't know the guards still replay dat tape of you to entertain demselves."

"Tape?" I feared someone had secretly taped me having sex in the office but didn't have a clue as to who made it. There were too many possibilities.

"De videotape of you in de parkink lot—"

"Videotape? They had that stuff back then?" I tasted vomit in my throat.

She shook her head in disgust. "Don't you ever think of de consequences of vat you do?"

"I was just a kid then, and a guy had hurt me."

"So, you put on a floor show for de security men?"

Why is she torturing me this way? "I won't make a fuss."

"You're lucky the Vermont reporter didn't have a camera. De newspaper article vas bad enough. Mona Lotte. Hah." She put her hands on her hips.

"I'll do something to get Ollie to break up with me tonight if you don't tell him these things." I blubbered, "Please, I'll do anything you ask." I fought the impulse to run but couldn't keep from sobbing.

Rose lifted my chin up so I could see her face. "Ollie doesn't need to know any of dis. I got around, too, but Bert doesn't know dat. I prdeli lot of guys in my time, but not a tend as many as you." She took a deep breath. "I have somethink you vant, and you have somethink I vant. Ve're in a perfect situation to strike a deal."

"I don't understand," I said between sobs.

"You have a great pelvis, and a few eggs dat still have a little shelf life. You can produce babies, if you get right to it. Ollie's sperm are also gettink old."

"You want grandchildren?" I quit sniffling and perked up.

"Bingo. And you're goink to get dem for me because you vant children. Right?" She stared, unblinking, into my eyes, waiting for an answer.

"More than anything. I don't feel complete without at least one."

"So, it's a deal den. Shake? You know dis means no other men until de kids are grown, don't you?" Her expression changed to one more congenial, but she was deadly serious.

I shook her hand. "I won't run around on Ollie. My kids aren't gonna come from a broken home."

"You realize, on your vedding day, you'll be gainink a son more dan a husband, don't you?"

I nodded, acknowledging the truth of what she said, as I dried my tears with the back of my hand.

"De men don't need to know anythink about dis, right? And Oliver can't know you're a charity píča, or he von't marry you."

"Right."

"Dry your eyes." She handed me a box of tissues. "Let's plan your veddink now."

"I'm very organized," I said, regaining my composure. "Here's what I think: marrying a year after meeting is about as short as I dare cut it without appearing impetuous or that I trapped him. Let's set the first Saturday after Labor Day for the wedding. I'll reserve my church for the service. We could get engaged on Valentine's Day and announce our wedding date along with the engagement."

"Know vat, my future daughter-in-law? Dat's exactly vat I was thinkink. Now, ve have to schedule your sex life."

CHAPTER 11

Operation Babymaker

How was I going to deal with a pervert for a mother-in-law who expected to control my sex life? "That's getting a little too personal, don't you think?"

Rose gave me an icy stare. "You vant to have a baby, don't you?"

"Of course I do." I couldn't believe she would think I'd have anything to do with her son otherwise.

"At your age, it isn't alvays easy. You've got to do everydink possible to stack de deck in your favor and, unfortunately, most of it has to do with Oliver's sperm count."

"Don't we just do it as often as possible until the rabbit dies?" I didn't expect it to be hard for me. I had gotten knocked up when I was taking serious precautions.

"Of course not. At his age, he can only produce so many sperms a day. Vorse yet, it takes him longer to re-build his stockpile after givink you vat he has at de time.

He should never have sex on consecutive days. Better even to have two days off in between."

"So, I give it to him once every third day then tell him to leave me alone? That doesn't sound realistic." I didn't have that much self-control. Sydney was going to be awfully busy.

"It isn't. Here's vat ve're going to do. You have sex vith him as much or as little as you vant until June. Den ve start Operation Babymaker."

"So, my job is to keep him interested until then. I'm just the woman to do that."

"So I hear." She sounded as supportive as she was disgusted with the kind of mother she thought she was getting for her grandchildren.

I gave her the thumbs up. "I have an approach in mind, but will modify it for the June launch."

"Startink in June, your primary objective becomes gettink pregnant as soon as possible. It might take a vile." She raised her eyebrows for emphasis.

"Isn't that a bit early? Shouldn't I wait until the wedding?"

Hell, with my luck, I might have to waddle up the aisle.

"Not unless you vant to reduce your chances. You need every advantage you can get."

"We might have a six-month baby?"

"Happens all the time. Don't vant Oliver to dink you trapped him because you got pregnant, do ve?" She held up her finger as she lectured me.

"No. I wouldn't show at the wedding and could wait

a month after it to 'find out.' The baby could be premature."

She winked, smiling like a Cheshire cat. "You got dat right."

"What will you be doing?" *While I'm teaching his sperm the breast stroke?*

"I'll be increasink your chances for success. First ding, I throw avay his briefs to cool his testicles to get his sperm count up. Dat needs to be done at least ten or eleven veeks ahead of your June start date."

"I could give him boxer shorts with hearts on them for Valentine's day." He'd look silly, but I'd make wearing them worthwhile.

Her smile gave way to a serious look. "He needs motivation to get married and be on his own."

"By doing everything for him, you make it awfully comfortable living here with you and Bert."

She gave me a dirty look then paused before speaking. "Ve'll change dat. Little by little, Bert and I vill make him less comfortable." She tapped her foot waiting for my response.

"While I make it inviting to be with me." I smiled, thinking of the fun I'd have with my daughter who will be the prize in this X-rated box of Cracker Jacks.

"Exactly. He also needs to be kept out of saunas, hot tubs, and very hot showers. Ve don't have a hot tub or sauna. I'll have Bert lower de vater heater temperature gradually so Oliver doesn't notice the shower gettink cooler."

I thought a couple of seconds before responding. "I'll

lower mine, too, in case he tries my place."

"Good. Every little bit helps." A small smile crept across Rose's lips.

"You know Ollie and I haven't had intercourse yet?"

Rose snapped her head to an abrupt stop and raised her eyebrows in disbelief. "I'm surprised, actually."

"Something else you probably won't believe is that I'm actually in love with him." I sold my soul to the devil, figuratively speaking, in exchange for a daughter. Rose had to think I held some feelings for her only son. At that point in my life, I would have agreed to anything, no matter how bizarre, if it got me a husband who would give me a little girl. I knew Rose wouldn't renege. She wanted a grandchild too badly to risk not getting one now that she was so close.

"I do believe you, but time will tell how long your love lasts."

The only sex Ollie had experienced with me so far were intense make-out sessions and increasingly better hand and foot jobs. With ten months to the wedding, I planned on steadily, but slowly, increasing his pleasure so he'd look forward enthusiastically to the honeymoon. It was past time to move from footjobs, to footjobs with nylons, and Ollie was pushing for a whole lot more. Normally, I enjoy acting out a man's fantasies but, to get my Mrs. degree, it was essential for Ollie to not know how experienced I was.

My problem was that my gynecologist was out of the country and I wouldn't trust anyone but her to mess with my IUD. It had to be out soon, or I might have caved when Ollie wheedled me for oral sex. If he got hooked on that, I might never get my little girl. Also, as terrific as I was, he might figure out I'd been around the block more times than a mailman. As soon as she returned and extracted it, Ollie could start coming inside me. Once it was removed, I'd insert sponges when we practiced for Operation Babymaker. When it was underway, I'd still excuse myself, without saying why, to make him think I was still using them.

❧

From the start, I advanced our relationship by doing things as a couple, not just as each other's dates. Rose backed me up at every turn. She "lost" the message whenever another woman called. She invited me along to family gatherings, no matter how distant the relationship. In short, she presented our marriage as a fait accompli to everyone. She always asked Ollie what we were doing, never what he had planned.

Rose—she insisted I call her by her first name—had held her son tightly all his life. Now, if she was going to have grandchildren, she had to hand him over to me. Aside from my past, I fit the daughter-in-law bill perfectly with no family in the area, my father dead, and my mother a thousand miles away without enough money to travel frequently.

She imagined my beautiful red-haired child standing out among her friends' grandchildren. Any objection Ollie raised warranted little serious discussion.

"What do you know? It's taken you almost thirty-five years to find someone."

Only occasionally, I arranged dates that weren't with other people. Most involved groups of people hiking, biking, attending an event, or going to a museum. Shortly after the IUD disappeared, I allowed Ollie to cook dinner for me at my place. He wore the smoking jacket I had given him for his birthday, and I wore my new, sexier lounging pajamas. I put on a Nat King Cole CD for background music and gave him my "come hither" look from my perch on the couch. Ollie jumped on me like a cat on a chipmunk. He had no experience with romance. The women he had been with wanted nothing more than casual sex.

Can't let this get started. I slapped his arms away. "Easy, boy. Can you be a little more romantic?"

"I don't know what it is about you, but I can't keep my hands off you tonight." He reached for me again.

I pushed back against his chest. "Try harder." When he relaxed, I demonstrated what I meant by kissing him gently. He kissed back hard. "Gently."

Ollie eased up. We made out nicely. He'd become proficient with my breasts. I gave him a gold star for that. However, he thought stars looked funny stuck to his forehead. My nipples enjoyed the attention, triggering me to moan and pull my top open farther to give him greater access.

"I want you. Now." He became insistent and jerked at my bottoms.

I grabbed hold of the elastic waistband, keeping him

from pulling them down. "You need to get me in the mood."

With me pantieless, only a thin layer of cotton shielded the target of his ardent desire. When I relaxed my grip, he had them down and off me in an instant.

I wasn't half as strong physically. I had to use my wits to stop him from taking me before the time was right.

"Whoa!" I cried, almost yelling at him. "Do you intend to make love or just fuck the shit out of me?" With that, I flopped back first onto the couch, flung my top wide open and spread my limbs as far as I could so he could take me like I imagined a Russian soldier takes a helpless woman who submits only to save her children's lives.

I dared him. "Come on, fuck me! That's all you want, isn't it?"

He tucked his tail between his legs like a dog that had been disciplined for misbehaving and started to leave.

I called after him as he grabbed the doorknob. "Don't go yet. We need to talk."

He slunk slowly toward me while I put myself back together.

"Here," I patted the couch. "Sit next to me."

He sat down, and I held his hands.

"I'm quite willing to make love to you any way you want. The problem is, you don't want to make love to me."

"Yes, I do." He looked quite confused sitting on the

edge of the couch as if he was on a straight-backed chair in the principal's office.

"No, you just want to fuck me. There's a huge difference."

"I do love you." He looked sincere, but as Clinton famously said, "Once you have the sincerity thing down, you've got it knocked."

"If you loved me, you'd treat me differently."

"How do you want me to treat you?" He looked like he was horny enough to do anything I asked.

"Simple. Move slowly and advance gently. If I like it, I'll encourage you. Got it?"

"I think so." He looked puzzled.

"Keep in mind I'm a woman and need to be seduced. I want it as much, maybe more, than you do, but I need you to want me, not just my pussy. Understand?"

He nodded.

"You may kiss me now."

Ollie did much better. I rewarded him for his improved behavior, but not necessarily how he wanted. I made sure he wouldn't suffer from blue balls, though.

"One thing before you go, ask your mother how to court a woman."

I gave him a pretty good smooch. "Goodnight." I pushed him gently toward the door. As soon as the door latched sounding his departure, I got into the shower. I don't know what pleased me more, my orgasm that night or the satisfaction of moving my relationship to a new level.

My battle plan called for me to delay Ollie on the

sexual front until he treated me better, while not frustrating him too badly. I never let him leave without relieving him in my diverse ways, often multiple times, but never oral sex. That was too addicting and therefore off limits. I fretted because he would soon be expecting it or intercourse ahead of my plan to wait until Valentine's Day, when he would be giving me my ring.

Providence interceded, for once in my favor. Ollie spent much of the next three months traveling around the country to his company's plants, causing him to be away on alternate weekends. I made a point of phoning him every night at nine and keeping him on the line until he was ready for bed.

His behavior improved after talking to his mother. He never grabbed me again. Ollie sent me cards occasionally and bought me little gifts to show he was thinking about me. Tim could've given him lessons in that regard. When I rewarded him for treating me better, he was most appreciative.

☙❧☙

Rose included me in Sunday dinners and family gatherings for Thanksgiving and Christmas, even when Ollie was away, as if I was already her daughter-in-law. In January, I had my engagement picture taken by a professional photographer before taking Ollie to a jewelry store to see a ring I really liked.

"It's simple: a solitary diamond in a white gold setting. I don't want anything ostentatious."

He looked puzzled. "Why are you telling me this?"

"It's time for us to get engaged or for me to move on. I'm not getting any younger."

"You mean you'll stop seeing me." A look of terror spread across his face.

"What's the point? If you don't care enough for me to want to fall asleep next to me every night and have breakfast with me in the morning, it's time both of us moved on."

Ollie put it on his credit card. On Valentine's Day, we went to a cozy cafe where we had a romantic dinner during which Ollie gave me a ring.

"It's beautiful!" I put it on my finger and ran around the table to kiss him. So happy was I that I lost control kissing him and almost knocked him over backward, chair and all, when I dry humped him.

"Ahem," said the maître d' I didn't see walk up. "Excuse me."

I turned to see him glaring at us in his tuxedo.

"Wow!" Ollie's eyes had glazed over from my smooch and the little extra from my hands.

"Here's your check." The maître d' handed me the bill and left before I could say anything.

I handed it to Ollie, saying, "Settle up while I get our coats. I've got a special present waiting for you at my apartment."

❧❧❧

Before taking my coat off, I handed him the phone. "Call your mother."

He took the phone but did nothing with it. "What should I tell her?"

"Tell her we're engaged—and you won't be home tonight. Fall weddings are best. The weather is neither too hot nor too cold."

After we both talked with Rose, I got out a small bottle of good Champagne I'd chilled for the occasion and handed it to Ollie.

Pop! He poured us each a glass.

"To us." I was so happy I would've done anything for Ollie.

We clinked glasses, and he drank his down. Seeing my glass almost full, he said, "You hardly tasted it. Is something wrong?"

"My body reacts so strongly to alcohol I can't risk losing control. Another?" I lifted the bottle to pour him another.

He put his hand over his glass. "About the present you promised me?"

"It's in the bedroom."

He rushed off to search my bedroom for his gift while I stored the Champagne bottle and washed the glasses.

Sounding let down, he said, "I don't see anything."

"You can't see it—yet, but you will soon." I put the apartment in order while he continued his search.

Finished with my chores, I joined him in my bedroom. "Here's a hint: Tonight, I give you what you want, any way you want it." *Except oral sex. Not till I'm pregnant.* "Take off your clothes and get in bed."

The telltale crinkling of cursed condom wrappers rattled my ears when he started undressing.

Can't let this get started. "You won't give me an incurable disease, will you?"

"Of course not. Why?" He looked really befuddled now, probably thinking I was reneging.

"I read that condoms reduce men's enjoyment," I said in my little girl voice, acting innocent.

"Yes?" He smiled, likely because he did enjoy it a lot more going bareback.

"I don't want to deny my husband anything, so I got some sponges for nights like this. I'll go put one in."

"You sure you don't want extra protection?"

"Not from you, darling." I tickled his tonsils with my tongue and pulled away. "Be right back." I winked.

Instead of giving him a floor show, I stripped in the bathroom. He needed to think I was inserting a sponge, but I had taken that precaution before dinner, just in case.

Ollie sat up in my bed, tapping his fingers impatiently, but soon I slid in next to him.

"You've got a head start," I said while making sure nothing covered his arousal.

His smile disappeared. "I thought tonight is the night."

"Just measuring your readiness quotient."

He moved to mount me.

I pushed him back. "You're marginally erect, and my readiness quotient hardly registers."

Pulling his hand to my breast, I said, "Get me so hot I'll want to act out your fantasies."

He complied to his limited ability. That night, I would have sizzled quickly with no external stimulus, but Ollie needed to be trained. Nothing he wanted required more than my C game. He tried nothing exotic. I let him lead and willingly participated. No passive sorority girl sex from me. Waking in the middle of the night unable to get back to sleep, I stroked him.

"Huh, what are you doing?" Although groggy, he was far from depleted from our earlier rounds and got ready as quickly as a cat could smell a tuna can being opened.

"I'm giving you a preview of what to expect on our honeymoon."

Apparently unaware of the existence of my clitoris, he fingered me in and out, but I didn't mind. When Little Ollie throbbed adequately, I climbed aboard and rode him like a cowgirl, practicing for when I'd be doing this spongefree. Ollie joined in the fun by trying to buck me off.

The *Star-Ledger* published our engagement announcement within two weeks, and I started making detailed plans for my wedding. My girlfriends and I shopped for dresses and shoes. Because Ollie and I were paying for most everything ourselves, I could've made most of the decisions. But I let Rose make many of them to keep her on my side.

My goal wasn't to have a Princess Di wedding. It was to have a daughter with her father's last name by getting myself pregnant as soon as humanly possible. All other things were minor details that mattered little. Bert arranged the rehearsal dinner as was customary in that area. Things moved right on schedule. Then, with only a few months left before the big day, my boss unexpectedly sent me to Las Vegas for a statisticians' conference.

CHAPTER 12

What Doesn't Happen in Vegas

I stormed into my boss's office after getting the memo ordering me to waste a week attending a useless statisticians' conference in Las Vegas. "You're pissing the company's money away," I said.

"It came down from on high. We have to send someone, and you've avoided it the longest."

It hurts too much to even think about returning. "You go then." I felt strong for standing up to a boss for the first time.

"It's too late for me to change my schedule."

"To go golfing at Hilton Head? My project will suffer."

"You're ahead of schedule as usual. Think of this trip as a reward for good work."

I straightened to maximum height and pulled my shoulders back. "I have a wedding to plan." *And you're trying to fuck it up, jerk.*

He picked up a folder and frowned at me. "Get out of

here before I get angry and make you stay for the second week. You'll love those thrilling meetings on bylaws changes."

"Damn you." I slammed his door on my way out.

His memo claimed the sessions would bring me current with the thinking in the field, but I found nothing in the program not already covered in detail in trade papers. I briefly considered poisoning his coffee, but the aftermath of that would disrupt my wedding plans even more.

Not only was he screwing up my wedding planning, he was sending me to a place it hurt to remember. After cooling down, I revised my matrimonial PERT chart, shifting forward as many tasks as possible. Starting them earlier offset the time that would be lost by being away for a week. My plan readjusted, I called my mother-in-law-to-be to break the news to her.

"I'm going to need your help, Rose. My damned boss is sending me away for a week, and I can't handle everything from there."

"Vere are you goink?" The tone of her voice had changed from the lilt when she recognized my voice to deadly serious.

"To a statistician's convention Las Vegas."

"Can't you get out of it?"

"I tried, but he won't let me." I pleaded for sympathy.

"You don't exactly have a good history. Dere vill be too many temptations."

"Don't you think I know that?" I was angry with her for rubbing my indiscretions in my face. "My baby's going to look like Ollie. I'm not going to screw up now."

"He better look like a carbon copy."

"With red hair. Can I count on your support?"

"Of course. Vat do you vant me to do?"

☙❧

Memories of the Las Vegas convention with Isaac haunted me. It had been the most spectacular week of my entire life. Going back would only cause me to relive the pain when he dumped me a week after we returned. In the Newark airport, I picked up a copy of *B is for Burglar* from the paltry book rack in the airport shop with the intent of distracting myself during the trip.

On the flight, however, I couldn't get my mind off much pleasure my Shanghai Squeeze, the cherry on top of a magical experience, had given Isaac. I felt good about myself for mastering this most difficult trick— learning it without going to a brothel for instruction. I considered my options for using it on Ollie. Reserving it as a reward for getting me pregnant, should it happen in my lifetime, might be a good idea.

On further thought, using it to get me knocked up sooner made more sense. Instead of sperms merely following their instinct swimming randomly inside me, hoping they'd eventually find my egg and fertilize it, I'd have thousands of them in a frenzy, all with a single purpose in mind—to be the winner of the impregnation lottery. The Shanghai Squeeze milked a higher percentage of his sperm into me with less waste and launched them deeper, closer to my egg seeking fertilization, thus improving my chances for success.

I decided to wait to tell Ollie about how Wallis Simpson "squeezed" her way to becoming the Duchess of Windsor until I returned from the trip. He had little to learn. All he had to do was to lie on his back, provide me with a throbbing hard-on and twiddle my nipples.

I planned on retraining my vaginal muscles in a miniskirt with nothing under it to facilitate quick reinsertion of the ivory egg until they were strong enough to hold it in place. Ollie would surely get off on popping it back in, but he'd have to wait for that phase of the plan. My IUD had only been recently removed, and it was six weeks to the date my plan called for doing him with my eggs welcoming all comers, so preparing to "squeeze" Ollie wouldn't be starting for a few weeks.

⁊⁊⁊

Preparing for this damned trip, I had made sure I was booked into a different hotel than before, but I was still melancholy walking through McCarran International after landing. Remembering how great it was in Vegas with Isaac brought back how badly it hurt when he left me for his wife. Choosing his community property over me after swearing undying love was a heartbreaker.

After checking in and depositing my junk in the room, I went downstairs for a light dinner. While I waited to be served in the packed dining room, the maître d' approached with a taller man behind him, examining me over his shoulder. The gaze from man's steel-blue eyes penetrated my soul.

My nipples jabbed at my unpadded bra in an attempt to bring themselves to the mysterious man's lips. I raised my eyebrows to the maître d'.

"There are very few empty seats, madam," he said, shrugging his hands and raising his eyebrows back at me.

"It's imperative I eat alone." I opened my wallet and took out a five.

"I'm sorry," said the maître d'. "You're sitting at a table for four."

"Move me then." I started gathering my things to change tables.

He motioned me to stay put. "There are no tables free now. The hotel is fully booked and too many people want to eat all at the same time." He pulled out the chair opposite me, signaling the end of the conversation. As he scurried away, his hand brushed against the man's hand as if they were hiding something.

The man standing across from me looked to be a couple of inches taller than me, with close-cropped dark hair having more than a few specks of gray, piercing dark eyes, trim, and was ruggedly handsome, wearing jeans and a blazer. He personified my dream man.

I didn't have to look down at my nipples to know I wanted him desperately. I was not impulsive, except when it came to men, but I didn't dare chance destroying my marriage, my last hope to have a daughter, before it got started.

"Hello. My name's Blake, and you are?" The

stranger gazed into my eyes with an air of more-than-modest confidence as he sat down.

I had to be on my guard. My name tag hid in my purse to keep lechers from knowing who I was and where I worked. Blake's nametag told me he lived too close to me for safety.

"Getting married in five months." I flashed my left hand just in case he had any ideas.

"Your first?"

Impertinent bastard. "Of course."

"What are you reading?" he asked, looking at my paperback.

"Just something to kill time." I put the book into my purse so he couldn't tell it was trashy.

"You look like someone who enjoys reading good books." He kept his eyes glued to mine, not wandering to survey my anatomy like most men do. "What is your favorite?"

"*To Kill a Mockingbird.* I reread it at least once a year."

"What is your favorite part?" His smile suggested that he appreciated my taste in books.

"It's hard to say," I stalled. "I like so much of it. Maybe Atticus's relationship with Scout." I hoped I didn't sound too gushy.

"Do you have a close relationship with your father?" He looked genuinely interested.

"I did," I said, holding back a tear that unexpectedly overcame me. "He died recently."

"What was that like?" He leaned in to hear me better.

Lightning bolts coursed through me from the tips of my fingers and toes straight to my groin, like the first time with Tim but a thousand times more intense. I wanted to take Blake right there on the table, but dared not. "Let's change the subject."

The waiter mercifully interrupted us by asking for our orders but, no sooner had he left than Blake started in again.

"I hope your marriage works out better than mine." He looked as if he'd lost his last friend.

Not another needy man. "What went wrong?" I straightened up to listen better.

"It's not what went wrong that matters now." He looked away as if he was trying to hide his vulnerability.

Might as well listen to his sob story. It'll keep him from talking about me. "Go on."

"It's my daughter. I really miss seeing her." His eyes misted when he mentioned her.

He hit my vulnerable spot like a laser. I couldn't imagine how painful it'd be to have a daughter and not be with her. "Don't you get visitation?"

"Her mother makes it difficult. Do you believe in second chances?"

"Not anymore," I said shaking my head. "Guys don't change."

"Not that kind of second chance. I mean a second chance at true love—with someone new."

Look out. He's going for the jugular—or something at the opposite end of my torso. "I suppose." *Saved by the bell.* The waiter arrived with our meals. "Bon appétit."

I shoveled it in, keeping my mouth full all the time, giving each bite at least ten chews to avoid conversing. However, it didn't stop Blake.

"I felt this—it's hard to explain—magnetic attraction to you. Instinctively, I knew you, like me, have been hurt badly by former lovers."

I had to watch myself because I'd never been so absolutely taken by a man before. I held up the palm of my hand while pointing to my mouth. Blake waited for me to respond but I pushed another forkful past my lips the instant I swallowed my cud.

Apparently seeing that he was getting nowhere, he ate the rest of his meal without speaking.

When I emptied my plate, he asked again, "Lovers have hurt you badly, haven't they?"

He sat silently waiting for me to finish chewing the last bite. I couldn't put him off any longer.

"They have, but now I'm engaged to be married." Needing to look strong, I showed my teeth when I smiled, something I rarely do.

"Tell me all about him." He smiled sweetly and relaxed in his chair as if he was listening to a great novel being read to him.

I told him the sanitized version about meeting Ollie five months prior and how our romance rapidly progressed, leaving out the collusion and planning with Rose or my fountain pen ruse. Blake interrupted only to offer support, make me laugh or compliment me. Only Tim had shown me this much attention, but his awkwardness spoiled the romance.

"Do you believe in love at first sight?"

I didn't know how, but he really knew me, how I'd suffered and how much I wanted to be loved. But I couldn't acknowledge believing in love at first sight, or I'd be finished. "Don't you think that's kinda silly?"

"It's not just your beauty, you're intelligent, too."

I had to change subjects to keep him from seducing me. "What brings you here?" I tried unsuccessfully to smirk.

"My boss."

"Mine too." I chuckled. "I really didn't want to come. It's a waste of time, and there's tons to do at home preparing for my wedding."

"We're fellow travelers, as it were."

The waiter brought the checks, letting me off the hook again.

After signing the check billing my room, I got up. "I think I'll stretch my legs for a while." I hoped he'd stay behind, while, at the same time, imagining what it'd be like with him.

"Mind if I accompany you to the corner?" He sounded innocent enough.

We strolled by the casinos for a couple of blocks along the strip.

"I thought you were walking to the corner."

"The corner down there." He pointed to a casino far in the distance. "Besides, I like to be seen with gorgeous women."

I flicked away his arm when he tried to put it around my waist.

"Have a nice walk." I tried to rid myself of him while wanting him to stay.

He took three steps then stopped abruptly and turned around. With a grin, he said, "I changed my mind."

I had to lose this guy before I bollixed my marriage big time. "I'm going back to the room to call my fiancé and get some rest."

He shook his head slowly. "He's a lucky guy to have landed you."

My heart fluttered, and my face blushed. "You're much too kind."

"Don't put on those pretensions of modesty. You know you're beautiful."

I'm not dropping my drawers tonight no matter how much I want to. I just can't. I could get pregnant or catch a disease.

Blake followed me to the elevator tower.

"Please don't follow me anymore." I jumped onto an elevator going up to thwart my desire to invite him into my room and body.

He reached out with both hands. "I don't know your name." The closing door may have clipped his nose.

The elevator's cocoon protected me from myself. As an extra precaution, I pressed random buttons above my floor to cover my trail.

Once in my room, I ran to the phone to call Ollie. *Drat.* It was too late to call without waking his parents. Damn time difference. I slept uneasily that night.

My plan was set. I'd marry the man I was engaged to and who would give me my daughter. My life was in perfect order. My mind raced. Why did Blake have to appear? Sure, the sex would probably be great, but would he marry me and give me children? Probably not.

I was glad I didn't give him my name, the company I worked for, or room number. He appealed to me only because I hadn't had an orgasm with a man in so long, I couldn't remember. That had to be it.

I mulled over having a fling to relieve my sexual tensions. Next week, I could attend to my pre-wifely duties, and this would all be forgotten. What if I fell in love with him? His company's office was within an hour's drive of mine. I could cheat with him easily. That would be too risky. My daughter was going to have a stable home. I fantasized I was with Blake while Sydney pleasured me.

The next morning, after an uneventful breakfast, I easily found my first session. I sat mostly asleep, daydreaming in the half-full conference room when my dreamboat sat down beside me.

"Tookie," he said, looking at my name tag, "is an unusual name. What's it mean?"

"Good morning." I tried to radiate ice as my heart raced.

"This session is boring. Which one are you going to next?"

"Sshhsss." I almost spat, trying to shut him up.

We sat quietly through the rest of the session.

"Like a cup of tea?" Blake asked to my back when I got up to leave.

"Sure." That sounded innocent enough, and I needed an energy boost.

He ordered Earl Grey, and I chose Red Zinger from the limited coffee shop selections.

"We're in the same track, I see from your nametag, and the rest of the sessions are worse than that one," he said. "Let's go to Lake Tahoe."

"I can't do that."

I bluffed. My boss would never know if I actually attended any sessions or not. A tryst in Lake Tahoe ranked pretty low on my outrageous behavior scale, but I was engaged to be married. I wasn't engaged to say I was engaged. I was getting married to have a baby. No way was I going to do something impulsive and risk missing out on having my daughter. I'd be thirty-five for almost two months, already a bit old to have my first child, thirty-six if I got pregnant in the first seven weeks. I knew I was fertile but how fertile?

I'd only been pregnant once, a very low success rate considering the number of copulations (sixteen active years at a hundred exposures per year, estimated conservatively by counting only Fridays and Saturdays and just once each date). It was hell being a statistician at times like that. I neared the end of my fertile years, and I dared not blow this last opportunity to have a daughter of my very own.

Blake took my hand, one of my weakest points because I love having my hand held. "Come on. It'll be our little secret."

"I'll meet you at the front door in ten minutes." *How'd that come out of my mouth?*

"I'll throw a few things in a bag and be waiting for you." He smiled broadly.

The bus to Lake Tahoe was far from full, with several rows completely empty. I picked the second of two adjacent empty rows.

"Sit there." I pointed to the window seat in the row in front of me.

"Why?"

"I don't want you to touch me, even accidentally, and I want you where I can keep my eyes on you."

"Okay, beautiful." He pouted. "It'll be tough on a seven-hour drive."

Seven hours? What had I got myself into?

I tried to enjoy the scenery on the ride, but my inner thoughts overwhelmed me. I was the female version of the mythological three-peckered billy goat and, to make matters worse, didn't bring sponges with me. I had no plans of having sex with anyone on this trip, so I didn't pack any. Getting pregnant would ruin everything. No way was I going to have another abortion. I was going to get married, get pregnant, carry my daughter to term, love her, take care of her, and love the grandchildren she gives me. I was not about to mess up my life. It took me decades to get to this point, and I wasn't going to blow it all for a little great sex. A million things raced through my mind.

Blake might not be divorced, or he could have had a vasectomy, or he could give me a disease that would make me sterile.

He checked in at the Cal Neva lodge, while a person

selling trinkets that might make appropriate gifts for my in-laws-to-be distracted me.

The desk clerk saying, "Next," got my attention.

Blake stepped aside and perused the trinkets while waiting for me.

My check in flowed quickly, too quickly, because it would put me in vulnerable territory, a hotel room, too soon. I paid in cash—no incriminating credit card trail. Finished, the desk clerk handed me the key.

"You're in room 206, Miss Lotte. It adjoins Mr. Kenlock's room."

Oh shit! I couldn't let him get away with this. I would be too tempted.

"No. That's not my room. I want one on a different floor that doesn't adjoin another room." I panicked inside but spoke as calmly as I could.

"I'm sorry for the mistake, miss. Here's the key to 407."

"Thank you. That should be fine." I sighed with relief, then turned to see Blake standing in front of me.

"Tookie, it's time for lunch. Meet you here in fifteen minutes."

"You can forget it after the stunt you just pulled." *Jerk.*

"I didn't ask for adjoining rooms." Blake raised his palms as if praying. "He just—"

"Bullshit. Get outta my sight." I turned my back on him.

"You've got to believe me. Just ask the desk clerk." He looked earnest for once.

"Don't make a scene." I believed him. I had overreacted on the clerk's mistaken assumption.

Apparently sensing a change, however slight, in my demeanor, Blake said, "Meet me here."

My defenses collapsed briefly. "Okay." *What harm could come from a simple lunch in a very public place?*

We ate a leisurely lunch in the coffee shop. I found myself opening up to Blake like I had to no man before. He asked me nonthreatening questions and listened attentively to my answers.

I talked a lot about myself, avoided the subjects of sex and mental health completely, and asked him a few questions.

He said little about himself. He was different from most men that way. My instinct told me to get away from him. I'd never be able to marry Ollie if I slept with Blake. He'd be so fantastic, I'd never want another man ever again.

"Gotta go now." I picked up my check and took it to the cashier.

Blake headed me off and snatched the check out of my hand. "My treat."

I plucked my check back out of his hand. "I'm on expense account."

"You can't submit. You're not supposed to be here." He pulled at my check, but I didn't let go.

"I get per diem. I don't have to itemize meals. Check and mate."

He let go as I pulled it back from him. He followed me into the casino attached to the hotel.

"What are you playing?" I had to get rid of him in a hurry.

"Roulette."

"It's that way." I pointed to a section in the far corner of the room, then headed off alone in the opposite direction.

I headed to the blackjack table and plunked down a ten-dollar bill for chips. I relaxed because I'd shaken him. My conservative system slowed my losses enough to last an entire hour at the table. The long bus ride, coupled with emotional angst, had exhausted me. I headed for my room feeling safe because I'd ducked Blake. But he caught up with me in the lobby.

"I'm going to my room for a nap."

"I'll join you."

"In your dreams. Meet me in the lobby at seven for dinner." *Where'd that invitation come from? I couldn't have said that.*

"And dancing?"

"If your feet can stand it." I was such a poor dancer, I lost several potential pickups back in my bar-banging days after stepping on their feet.

I got back to my room at a quarter after two. Ollie would be home from work in a few minutes. After freshening up a bit, I put Blake out of my mind and made my obligatory calls, starting with Rose.

"Greetings from Nevada." I felt safe from myself in another world when I heard her voice. My confidence in her making this wedding happen helped me through the ordeal.

Talking about trivialities took my mind off my dilemma.

Rose answered. "Vat time's it dere? It's five-dirty here."

"It's two twenty-five here now." Rose had set her clock five minutes fast so she wouldn't be late but was anyway. "How's everyone?"

"Bert's got a cold and Oliver's complainink about the vater temperature."

We both giggled.

"How're the arrangements going?"

"Ve have to decide on the main course."

"I don't know. Fish or chicken. Which would you prefer?" While some brides focused on extraneous trivia for their coronations into wifedom, I kept my eyes on the prize. Hell hath no punishment to compare with an unhappy, domineering mother-in-law.

So, I did everything in my power to keep her on my side. We'd have goulash for the main course if she liked. I wanted her son's sperm and name for my baby. Those were what mattered. She could decide most everything else except my wedding gown. That one thing was reserved for my girlfriends and myself. We'd bond as we shopped for it.

"Bert likes whitefish, but I don't care much for fish."

"Chicken it is then."

"Here's Oliver. He just got home."

"Thanks. Can you let the caterer know?"

"Let the caterer know what?" asked Ollie.

"Tell her to let the caterer know we've chosen chicken, darling." Sentimentalities made him uncomfortable, so I teased him with them.

"How's your conference, beautiful?" he jabbed back, punching me in my insecurity about my looks.

"I hate it. The sessions are boring."

"It'll be over in a few days."

"My next session starts soon," I lied.

"Love you."

"I love you, too." I had convinced myself that I loved Ollie, at least enough to marry him.

That chore taken care of, I rested until time for dinner, with rested being a relative term. I desired Blake more than any man before him, but acting on that desire would jeopardize the possibility of ever having a daughter of my own.

Not acting on it would leave me wondering what might have been. Would I be passing up the love of my life or would I just feel dirty afterward? My quandary thwarted my napping. No one could help me. I dared not share any of this to get advice.

I decided to test Blake at dinner by wearing my off-brand jeans and a button-front blouse that made me look flat (I usually wore it under a sweater). I looked anything but beautiful when I met him in the dining room.

"You look absolutely scrumptious tonight."

Liar, liar, pants on fire. "Will you marry me, Blake? I'm deadly serious."

CHAPTER 13

To Screw or not to Screw

W hat kind of question is that?" Blake contorted his face before responding.

"You want to sleep with me, don't you?" I asked, never more serious about anything.

"Well, ah, ah. I've never been taken by a woman anywhere close to this much before," he said as drops of sweat beaded on his forehead.

"I need to know if you will marry me before I let you make love to me."

"That makes no sense at all, Tookie."

"Will you give me a baby, two if the first one isn't a girl?" I remained deadly serious.

"That makes even less sense." His brow furrowed and his pupils narrowed.

"I have to know."

"I don't know you well enough."

"You know me well enough to dip your pen into my inkwell." *Quit dodging, you bastard.*

"What we do here can stay here."

"Not if you knock me up," I said with my quietest little girl voice.

He gulped. "You're not on the pill or something?" His look changed to one of disbelief.

"I'm having a baby as soon as I can, and she has to look like my husband, whoever that turns out to be." My voice surprised me by regaining some of its strength.

"You're asking for a huge commitment."

"Oh, and you're not?" I sighed. "I'm just not as special to you as you say."

"You want too much, Tookie. Have a nice evening." He turned to leave.

"This town's loaded with chapels. They all sell fucking licenses."

Blake threw up his hands and left as fast as his feet would carry him.

After eating dinner alone and not wanting to return to the boring conference in Vegas, I needed to find something to do in Tahoe.

The brochures in the hotel lobby about local attractions offered a couple of interesting possibilities. Looking through the flyers didn't take long, so I swung by the casino and took the first open seat at the blackjack table.

Shit. I should've checked out the dealer before sitting down. Maybe this will change my luck. The butchish dealer dealt me a jack and a ten. I held pat. She dealt herself and ace and a queen. *So much for changing my luck.*

Getting worse cards than usual, I played only a few hands before exhausting my chip supply.

Losing my daily limit too quickly, I strolled back to the hotel to look over their sundries shop. I picked up a copy of *Glitz* and extra batteries for Sydney. I'd been wanting to read Elmore Leonard for some time but, for reasons unknown, hadn't gotten around to it. Now, I had a few days to fill. After reading a couple of chapters in my room, I perused the brochures, picking hiking for the next morning's activity. I worked Sydney overtime that night, needing to have a negative horniness quotient in case I ran into Blake again.

The next morning, I hiked among the spectacular scenery surrounding Tahoe until dense fog blocked my view of the mirror-like lake and made further trekking unsafe. I envisioned myself as Greer Garson (I have the hair if not her looks and bearing) in her big scene from *Goodbye Mr. Chips,* but I didn't want a fuddy-duddy like Chipping finding me. I called, "Halloo," a few times, hoping for an answer, but Blake didn't reply. Following in Garson's footsteps, I pulled my paperback out of my bag and sat still until the sun broke through. When hiking was safe again, I trekked back to the lodge, taking in the breathtaking valleys that had been carved out of the mountains by receding glaciers. Arriving back at the hotel at noon chilled from the cold dampness at high altitude, hot chocolate never tasted so good. After a quick lunch, my bed beckoned. I was safe in my cozy, rustic room. Blake wouldn't dare knock on my door.

I spent the rest of the afternoon reading *Glitz,* dozing, and calling Ollie and Rose. I woke from my nap too late to make dressing for dinner worth the bother. Splurging on room service for the luxury of eating in my pajamas felt as decadent as not having to leave the room or worry about encountering Blake "by accident." I no longer slept nude in hotels after an embarrassing incident involving a false fire alarm.

On my last full day in Tahoe, I toured the town in the morning. The stops included a wedding chapel and a divorce ranch. For the afternoon's entertainment, I suffered through a thirty-mile bus ride to take in the nearest brothel. The madam must have had some intuition about women's abilities to please men because she offered me—not one of the prettier women on the tour—a job. That evening, I dressed for dinner, wearing the simple black dress, I had bought a few years earlier to have something to wear when slacks weren't appropriate. Flats, comfortable underpants, bra but no cursed pantyhose finished off my outfit.

I enjoyed a healthy meal, eating all the vegetables, but only half the meat. Afterward, I lost my ten dollars to the casino more quickly than desired, leaving me time for a dance or two. "Can't Find This Feeling" led me into the ballroom, where a top 40s band wearing tacky maroon jackets played for a quarter-filled room. I immediately saw what I wanted, an empty table near the dance floor. To make it better, well-dressed older gentlemen were seated nearby. I had read where casinos hired them to entertain gamblers' wives.

They would surely ask me to dance a time or two, expecting nothing in exchange.

Even before the next song started, a trim man with

salt and pepper hair wearing a tailored gray business suit approached. Extending his hand and smiling, he asked, "Would you like to dance, miss?"

"That's what I'm here to do." I took his hand to let him help me out of my chair, even though assistance wasn't needed.

He led me to a vacant part of the floor to wait for the music to start. "Is this your first trip to Reno?" He asked in the manner of a tour guide trying to break the ice.

The band started playing, making conversation impossible. So, I just nodded and wiggled my body in time to the music.

He was quite graceful, as I'm not, but I do like shaking my body around the dance floor occasionally—better when no one I know can see me. His courtly manners put me at ease. Rationing my partners to two consecutive dances to catch my breath, I sat out the third song. Just as the tune started, a familiar voice spoke from behind.

"May I have the pleasure of this dance, Tookie?"

Shit. "I hoped you'd given up."

He walked around and faced me with his hand outstretched.

"Only one." I had to limit my exposure to him to keep from weakening.

"I'll take whatever you'll give me." He gave me a small smile.

Blake danced marginally better than I did. That gave me some consolation. I turned toward my chair during the last note.

"Let me have another. That was too short."

I felt obligated because that one barely lasted two minutes. "Okay."

When "Private Dancer" started, he embraced me.

Can't risk this. "No slow dances." I wriggled free and walked off the dance floor.

He grabbed my wrist. "Why not? You danced one with that other guy." He sounded more than a little irritated.

"Because I can't trust myself." I tore free and raced out into the hallway, shoes slipping on the heavily waxed marble floor.

Blake caught up with me in the lobby and grasped my hand. "Please talk to me."

"Out there where it's cooler." I pointed toward the veranda and turned my back on him as I walked. "You can continue talking, but I can't look at you." I tried to protect myself from myself. I didn't hear a thing Blake said. I heard sounds over the music which flowed out of the ballroom, across the lobby, and out where we stood, but I couldn't process words.

All of a sudden, his warm hands cupped my breasts from behind, and his hot lips seared the back of my neck.

"You know you want me." He rubbed his desire against the top of my bottom.

"Please stop. You're too hard to resist." I wished there were people out there with us. Unable to control myself, I leaned back into him to better feel his erection poking me.

He flicked my already erect nipples through my dress and unpadded bra, causing me to melt. As the song stopped, he tried to turn me around. I resisted by holding his hands in place. Blake countered by nibbling on my neck and ears while twiddling my nipples.

When "Everything She Wants" started, he began sliding his hands down my front at a slow, sexy pace. Not wanting to waste any more time, I pushed them to my flaming red triangle, where we both wanted them to be. His fingers found my on button as easily as if he had a road map for my body. The thin layers of cloth from my dress and lightweight tricot panties didn't impair his ability to navigate my nether regions.

"Ooooooohhhh." My moans of desire blended into the music.

He surprised and frustrated me by not bringing me to a quick climax. Blake toyed with me, only occasionally brushing my clit. Instead of hurrying to get me off, he combed my hair with curled fingers.

"It's great that you're natural and haven't shaved away your womanness."

I can't even imagine shaving there. I grabbed his fingers to put them where they'd do me the most good.

He resisted, whispering, "You know you want me." Blowing his hot breath down my neck only excited me more.

I moaned louder and plastered my back to his front, writhing with anticipation. He teased me more by sliding his hands down and up my inner thighs. When he finally flicked it, I drenched myself.

I forced myself to stand still to soak in the attention he was giving me. The longer I did, the less rational I got.

I wanted to kiss Blake, but I was afraid my blazing lips would scorch him.

Unable to control myself any longer, I turned around, wallpapering his body with mine, and put my arms around his neck.

Just as "The Heat Is On" began, he pressed his powerful, nubby fingertips firmly along either side of my spine. Slowly massaging my back, veneering my burning body to his, he pushed his hands down my backbone, vertebra by vertebra, past my tailbone, and cupped my cheeks in them. He pulled me so tightly against him, I became a second smoldering skin.

I couldn't pull away. All I could do was kiss him on the neck. Hard. And with so much passion, I left a hickey, something I had always religiously avoided doing.

"Ouch." His shoulders flinched, and he pulled me even more tightly against him, pressing his throbbing, rock-hard baby maker against my belly.

I pulled down against his neck raising my body up to align us perfectly. Taking my hint, he lifted my ass with his powerful hands and pressed my sizzling box against his throbbing thumper. Oooh, it felt so good. I'd always loved feeling a man's desire prod me, starting with the first time Tim hugged me all aroused way back when.

I couldn't control myself. I let go, certain Blake wouldn't drop me, hiked up my dress, and wrapped my legs around him. I dry humped with a desire I'd never had for a man before, panting, unable to catch my breath. He carried me the short distance across the veranda, through a door, straight to an open elevator off the lobby.

A woman our age scowled at me as I grinded him all the way to the elevator.

"Quit gawking! I bet you've never given a man a time to compare with what I'm gonna give him the second we reach his room—sooner if the elevator's slow."

She turned her red face away.

I pressed the button for his floor and stuck my tongue far down his throat, kissing him passionately until he gagged, easing up only to let him breathe. Just then I saw myself on the mirrored walls of the elevator. I'd never gotten a really good look at myself in action before. I was more exciting than those cheesy porn queens. Maybe we should make a movie.

"Let me down," I demanded.

He complied, seemingly overwhelmed by my passion.

I pushed my soaked Thursday panties off my hips, wriggled them down to my ankles, then kicked them free. "I want you now."

Ding. The elevator stopped, and the doors opened.

"Press the hold button." I tugged at his belt buckle. "Take me here, right now!"

"Too late." Blake led me out of the elevator by the hand past some half-drunk conventioneers who were getting on as we got off.

One of them picked up my panties and twirled them around. "Red, you sure these aren't your mother's?" Girls had teased me about not wearing bikinis in high school, but these felt better on me.

I laughed as Blake pulled me down the hall. "Keep

them as a souvenir." Memories were what I desired.

The one who was twirling my damp scanties held them to his face. "From their smell, I'd guess Red's ready to vault his pole." They all laughed.

I threw my admirers a kiss as Blake trotted me to his room. He quickly unlocked and pushed me through the door, firmly but not rough. When he reached for the light switch, I pulled his hand away.

"Open the drapes. The city lights are more romantic."

He complied, then kicked off his shoes and started unbuttoning his shirt.

Out of habit, I put my glasses in my purse and hung it on the doorknob before walking toward the bed. I kicked off a shoe with each step then sat at the foot, wriggling, my pulse racing for him to have his way with me. Looking up, I noticed the mirrored ceiling over the bed and imagined camera shots of my reflection giving Blake world-class oral sex. My body would block the shot if he was lying on his back. Me on my knees with him standing on the bed wouldn't work. He'd bang his head on the ceiling. Both lying on our sides would show my face best.

When he finished taking off his shirt, I hiked up my dress and motioned him to come hither, spreading my legs wide for encouragement, not that he needed any.

Now panting, I unbuckled his belt and jerked down his zipper, then, in one motion, pulled his slacks and briefs down below his knees.

Between gasps, I ordered, "I wanna see you naked."

He jumped out of his slacks and briefs and reached for me.

"Socks too. This isn't a porno movie." *Yet.*

He pulled them off and slid me back onto the bed.

Sweltering in the air-conditioning, I thrust my arms straight up toward the mirrors. "Take it off. I want you to see me."

Instantly, he had my conservative black dress over my head and sailing off onto the floor.

Noticing how bizarre I looked in the mirror above his bed, naked except for my brassiere, I said, "*All* of me," and reached behind my back to unhook it.

He girdled me with both hands and deftly swept it away more quickly than I could. He grasped me by my uncontrollably gyrating hips and skidded me on my simmering bottom up the sheet so my head rested on a pillow. He pulled out a condom and started opening the wrapper.

I slapped it out of his hand. "No! It'll melt. I'm so hot." I wanted Blake so desperately I thrashed wildly on the bed, panting, seized with a passion more intense than any lover had brought me before.

He took an ankle in each hand, spread me wide open, and hopped up onto the bed, landing on his knees between my splayed legs.

"Hurry. Damn it. I can't wait any longer."

As he scooted forward to bisect my triangle, I grasped his pulsating impregnator, rammed it into me, and heaved my hips up to embed him deeply in my womb.

"Oooohh." *This is the best ever. What if I don't get pregnant? What if I do? What if he won't marry me? I can't go back to Ollie pregnant.*

I panicked. "No! This is so wrong." I threw Blake off me with all my might, screaming, "Nooo, I can't do this." Hysterical, I rolled off the bed, grabbed my purse, and ran out of his room. Halfway to the elevator, I realized I was stark naked and grabbed a bath towel off a house-keeping cart. I covered as much of me as I could.

In my room, I took a scalding hot shower, douched, and brushed my teeth in an attempt to cleanse myself. I put on my pajamas and bathrobe, rechecked all the locks, wedged a chair against the door, took the phone off the hook, closed the drapes, turned out the lights, and crawled into bed. I cried, shivering with cold sweat much of the time. Eventually, I fell into a deep sleep.

When my alarm went off in the morning, I frantically dressed, packed, and nibbled a quick breakfast in the coffee shop, wanting to get away from Tahoe as soon as possible. I walked the short distance to the bus stop, relieved that Blake was out of my life for good. But when I stepped onto the bus, I saw him. I scoured the bus, but the only empty seat was next to him.

He moved a large sack from the seat and patted it.

I didn't anticipate this. What could I do?

"Tookie, what happened to you?" He looked completely puzzled.

"Don't talk to me, please." *What if he blackmails me? I haven't saved much money.* "You probably bribed the band."

A small grin escaped from his look of earnestness. "I love you. I want you more than any woman ever. Please don't do this to me."

He tried to put his arm around me but I pushed it away.

"I'm getting married and having a baby. You can't be in my life." I slid as far from him as I could without falling out of my seat.

His shoulders slumped at my words.

"We only live an hour apart. Please." All energy had dropped from his face.

"No. No. No. It's over. Done. Finished." I was now angry at him for his insistence.

He shook his head. "I'll call you in a month."

"Don't ever contact me again." I turned away from him.

Blake handed me a paper bag containing the clothes I left in his room.

Knowing those reminders of Tahoe would haunt me forever if they were in my house, I let the bag fall to the floor and left it there.

At the airport, I checked in for my flight, then looked for a pay phone. I pushed in every coin I had on me and dialed Rose's number. Ollie answered.

"Can you pick me up at the airport, dear? I'll make it worth your while if it's inconvenient."

"Sure."

"Give my best to your mother. Tell her you're staying over tonight, all weekend if you're good. Love you."

I couldn't waste any more time worrying about Blake now. I had to get myself big with pig.

CHAPTER 14

Going to the Chapel

On the flight home, I filled my mind with work-related minutia, so I wouldn't think about what I ached to do—and almost did—setting those concerns aside until later. While sipping a cranberry juice, I re-read the session descriptions, all of which could be summarized as nothing I didn't already know.

At the conference, I'd made a point of observing the people my boss would ask about—from a distance, of course—mentally recording any new tic or behavior, including changes in attire, from which to conjure answers to his probable questions.

I determined how I could cut off the conversation if he was about to blow my cover. I'd ask him if he'd ever been to The Chicken Ranch. Everybody in the office knew his wife would dump him in a second in favor of her boyfriend if she could prove he'd been to a whorehouse. If he persisted, I'd tell him The Chicken Ranch manager offered me a job when I toured the place—but not as a statistician—and for a lot more money than he paid me. He hated talking about salaries.

Knowing where I worked from my conference credentials, made it easy for Blake to contact me. He phoned several times before I started letting them go into voicemail. He reacted by writing me beautiful love sonnets. His words made my heart and loins ache, but I dared not act on my impulses.

I focused on two things: managing my wedding, and ensuring a little girl grew in my womb as quickly as possible—my wedding night wouldn't be soon enough. I started going into the office at seven a. m. to get my important tasks completed in the three to four hours before wedding-related interruptions took over.

Ollie's parents insisted on paying the things that traditionally were the groom's parents' responsibility. I paid for my wedding myself. Mother couldn't, so I didn't ask.

Picking out my wedding dress at Princess for a Day brought back fond memories. They had numerous beautiful gowns, any number of which would have looked fine on me. But I chose one reminiscent of my first communion dress. On that beautiful spring morning when Daddy saw me in it, he exclaimed, "You look like an angel about to ascend to heaven." He loved me so much. I missed him terribly. He was wonderful to all of us, but I was his favorite.

My girlfriends humored me about the dress, saying, "It's your day. Wear what you want." I let them pick out the shoes. I wanted white flats. Evelyn handed me one-inch heels. I acquiesced.

In the summer, Mom and Daniel flew in from Arkansas, supposedly for a vacation, but actually to give Ollie the once-over. He drove me to the airport to meet their flight.

As we walked from the parking lot to the terminal, he said, "You owe me. I wanted to play golf this morning."

Ollie always whined when asked to do anything that inconvenienced him.

"Don't worry. I'll make it up to you." I rubbed his crotch to make the point. "Haven't I always?"

"No denying that, but let's make this as quick and painless as possible. Okay?" He stepped up the pace.

We arrived as their jet pulled up to the gate. A few minutes later, they emerged from the jetway.

For the first time, I noticed Mother had aged considerably since Dad died. Widowed at sixty-one, she considered herself too old and tired to consider remarrying or even dating. Although she had cut down her drinking dramatically, its effects from those decades of swilling beer every night had taken their toll. She had been shorter than me since my early teens, but she was even shorter now. She'd shrunk. I didn't take after her at all, not just in height and shape; my oval face was nothing like her round one. My red hair and, I think, freckles came from Dad's side.

Daniel just looked after Mom and played chess. Not much else. Never working a real job, he was content having no money or possessions and few friends. All he wanted to do was pursue an amateur chess career.

"Mother, this is Ollie, my fiancé." I held a tiny bit of hope she'd like him, but he didn't help his case by looking bored to be there. "Ollie, Mother."

"Hello, I hope you had a nice flight." His words were right but slouching like a spoiled teenager wasn't likely to ingratiate himself to his soon-to-be mother-in-law.

For an instant, Mother let her feelings of disgust show but then quickly masked them. "I'm so glad to meet you at last, Ollie. Mary Louise told me all about you." Her posture told me she didn't like him.

I hugged Daniel before introducing him. "Ollie, this is my chess-master brother, Daniel." He recoiled noticeably when Ollie shook his limp hand.

The drive home was awkward. My questions and comments elicited nothing more than one-word responses from any of them. Coming to an abrupt stop in front of my apartment, Ollie looked at his watch and lied, "I'm running late." He deposited us and their bags on the sidewalk and drove off without even kissing me goodbye.

Somehow keeping a straight face, Mother said, "Tim would have carried our bags in for us, Mary Louise."

"He was late for an important meeting," I said.

They looked unconvinced. We picked up the suitcases and walked silently in.

Mother looked impressed as she scanned the living room. "This's much nicer than where you lived the last time I visited."

"I make more now and can afford something fairly nice." I motioned for them to take seats on the floral couch.

Daniel remained standing, looking belligerent. "He's a creep. He just wants you for sex."

"That's not true. He really loves me." *If he doesn't now, he will after our honeymoon.*

Mother looked up from her seat on the sofa. "Mary Louise, as much as I hate to say it, Daniel might be right."

"If he cared for you at all, he'd treat you better," said Daniel, out of character. Ordinarily, Mike was the brother who protected me.

"He treats me fine." I wracked my brain for a new topic to redirect the conversation to.

"Compared to who? Not Tim, that's for sure."

"You don't know anything, Daniel."

"Now, Mary Louise, think about what you're saying." Mother crossed her arms and glared at me. "Would Tim have dumped us on the curb and pulled away without even kissing you goodbye?"

Mom always liked Tim and delighted in pointing out how I let him get away.

I straightened up so I could look down at her. "But I don't want Tim. I want Oliver."

She stepped closer, crowding her face in mine. "You didn't answer my question, Mary Louise."

"No, he wouldn't." I crumbled under her pressure.

"Would you have children today if you'd married him?"

"Too many probably." That was the excuse I gave Tim whenever he talked marriage.

"You know better than that. Women control when

and how many children they have these days." My mother wouldn't accept my argument without including her stock, "In my day, women submitted to their husbands and, if it was God's will, they had babies."

"Besides, he's married now."

"Who, Ollie?" Daniel said, raising his palms. He always had trouble following conversations because he didn't pay attention.

Irritated by his impertinence, I snapped, "Tim, of course. He got married five years ago, didn't he?"

"Yes, but most marriages don't last that long these days. You could call him." Daniel looked sincere. He'd never bonded with Tim but didn't dislike him.

"Don't know his number."

Daniel squinted, then said, "Ask Information. He lives in the same place."

"You marry him. Or you, Mother. You always liked him, and you're single now."

"Your father and I liked Tim because he was madly in love with you and would've done anything to make you happy."

If I was going to marry anybody else, it would have been Blake, not Tim. And I didn't want anyone to know Blake existed, let alone how close I came to letting him father my daughter.

"I'm marrying Ollie, and we're going to have at least one red-haired baby, and that's the end of that."

Seeming resigned to me marrying Ollie, Mother said, "At least he's better than that good-for-nothing creep your sister married."

"He was good at one thing," Daniel said with a chuckle. "Impregnating women."

Years earlier, Mother and I had gone down to Richmond to help Beth birth her baby. She labored for hours as her doofus husband dashed in and out of her room, not staying long each time.

Smelling a rat, I positioned myself in an alcove from which I saw everything happening in the hallway without being seen, while Mother tended to Beth.

Eventually, he emerged from Delivery Room One and entered Delivery Room Three, where Beth was. With little happening at the time, he left and returned to Delivery Room One.

I peeked into that room when someone else entered. The One Whose Name I Shall Not Say held the hand of a girl a few years younger than my sister. That bastard had two women in labor at the same time! It was like a bad Dudley Moore movie. No way was my life going to be like hers. Smirking, I said, "I'm very pleased you consider Ollie better than that."

I showed them the guest bedroom and opened the closet. "Mother, how do you like my dress? Does it remind you of something else?"

"Oh yes. It's like your first communion dress. You'll make a beautiful bride."

Daniel pointed at my dress and frowned. "*You*'re wearing white?"

"Mother. Where's he get off? He's never even had a date. Girls who get around a lot more than me wear white these days."

Mother glared as she shot daggers at her oldest son. "Daniel, don't start."

He retreated to the kitchen where he set up his chess board on the little table and ignored us until it was time to eat.

I drove the three of us to Charley's Other Brother's Place to meet Ollie for dinner. On time, we got out of the car and walked to the front door, expecting Ollie to be there. He wasn't.

Daniel raised himself on his tiptoes to scan the parking lot. "I thought you said he'd be waiting for us here. I'm hungry."

"He must have gotten stuck in traffic." I looked at my Seiko from Tim to check the time. "We better go in so we don't lose our reservation."

Inside, the maître d' led us to a table by the kitchen.

In an attempt to salvage the evening as best I could, I did something out of character for me. "Could we have a quieter table?"

He glared at me. "There's nothing available right now."

"That's okay," I said in my cheeriest voice. "We can wait."

Daniel poked me in the side. Annoyed, I slapped his hand away. "You'll survive."

We returned to the waiting area and took seats on the bench there. Muzak added to, rather than covering up, the noise of the other eaters.

Daniel stopped fidgeting and crinkled his nose. "The smell of those steaks grilling has whetted my appetite."

Ollie arrived, and a few minutes later another table came free, ending the need for smalltalk.

I felt good about myself for being assertive after the pompous maître d' left us at a far better table. I passed around the menus to give everyone an excuse for not talking.

Daniel flipped back and forth through the large pages, grunting occasionally. "Don't they have burgers?" he asked.

"Only if you sit at the bar," Ollie said, shifting his gaze across the room.

"Stay here, Daniel," I said. "Have something nice for a change. This's on me."

During the meal, I guided the conversion to the food, the safest topic I could think of.

"Everything is good here, but I never order the scampi." I caught Ollie's eye when I slipped my hand under the table and rested it on his lap. "Ollie has spoiled me. His is so much better than any I've ever had in a restaurant."

Ollie looked even more uncomfortable when I stroked Little Ollie just enough to arouse him.

Outside the restaurant after paying the bill, I handed my keys to Mother. "Ollie and I have some details to iron out that won't wait. Drive my car home. He'll drop me off when we're finished."

Mother and Daniel looked at each other, surprised I was leaving them alone.

Ollie's look changed from puzzlement to a smile when he realized what I had in mind.

"Where to?" he asked when we'd gotten into his car.

"Wherever you want." I checked the time on my watch. "You've got me for forty-five minutes."

"I know just the place. Get ready while I drive."

I had my slacks and bra off and his pants opened by the time he pulled into a dark parking spot behind a near-by closed business. Stolen moments like these took the edge off during their visit.

Knowing he wasn't cut off probably made Ollie more pleasant to them, but Mother's and Daniel's opin-ions of him improved little. No further friction was ob-served before they returned to Arkansas.

With them gone, I continued making arrangements. Our—Rose's and my—plan called for rationing Ollie's sex until the honeymoon while gradually ramping up his pleasure factor. I stopped using sponges on June first and intentionally omitted them from my packing list. The thought that I might get pregnant increased my pleasure quotient which, in turn, increased Ollie's. He had one helluva good summer. He got me less often but, when he did, I gave him close to my best.

In between, I overworked Sydney so badly, I had to replace him. The upside of needing a new vibrator was seeing all the new toys at my favorite sex shop.

Focus. You're here to get a new vibrator. Nothing else. Ooohh. The Eruptus 7 will be just the ticket. Will he be Sydney III or IV?

I handed my new toy to the check-out clerk. "Where's the restroom?"

He glared. "Cash or credit."

"You're no fun." I drove home as fast as I dared to try out my new toy.

Rose and I planned Ollie's fatherhood to the minutest detail. I convinced her she wasn't losing her son, she was gaining a daughter and, hopefully, a granddaughter. She kept him away from me when necessary to keep his sperm count up, never allowing Ollie to see me two days in a row, except when I was ovulating—every third day most of the time. This wasn't a chore for Rose. She enjoyed having her son around. Ollie didn't complain. He had more time for golf and hanging out with his buddies.

By keeping Ollie away so much, Rose gave me more time to arrange the wedding. More importantly, it was integral to my sex-rationing plan. Only seeing him twice a week meant he got me almost every time he saw me. He was finicky about having sex with me when I had my period, so I smoked his cigar those nights. He never complained about that.

I gave myself to him most generously when his sperm count was high and avoided contact when it wasn't. I made it worth his while to stay over the nights I ovulated. It didn't take Ollie long to figure out how great a time he'd have when I was enthusiastic and not so much if I wasn't, so he adjusted his golf schedule around my cycles.

I honored Evelyn, my good and enduring friend, by selecting her to be my maid of honor. Evelyn wasn't very tall. She was really short. It was hard to find bridesmaid dresses well proportioned for someone her height, so I let her pick out the style for hers. We compromised on the color. I wanted green, of course, but she wanted red. It accentuated her blonde hair extremely well. She had to look gorgeous. I invited the guy she was dating and wanted to marry. If seeing her looking like this didn't sway him, nothing would.

Mother, my emotionally distant older sister Beth, and baby brother Jack crammed into my apartment for the wedding. Daniel and Mike stayed away. Mike, who "protected" me from Tim, disliked all my boyfriends.

Everything went smoothly until the rehearsal the evening before the service. My charismatic, but nondescript middle-aged minister grinned as he scanned the group assembled to see who was present. First weddings happened too late in life these days to suit him, and he officiated second, third, and fourth nuptials less than enthusiastically. I tuned him out when he got too preachy.

"Mary Louise, the blushing bride." He smiled at me. "Tomorrow, the bells ring in your honor. Where's the groom?"

"Here." Ollie raised his hand.

"The best man?"

"Over here," said Ollie's formerly slim college buddy.

"The matron of honor?"

"It's *maid* of honor," said Evelyn from out of sight, behind Mother, Beth, and me.

"Could I see you, please?" he asked.

Evelyn worked her way around us. "Here I am."

"Mother of the bride?"

"Here," Mother said, looking less than overjoyed.

"Mother of the groom?"

"Here I am, here," exclaimed Rose, beaming ear-to-ear, almost bouncing.

"Father of the bride?"

My eyes started watering without any warning. I tried to hold back the tears, but they flowed uncontrolled down my cheeks. Mother held me the first time since I was a teenager, patting my back and stroking my hair. Until that moment, I didn't realize how much it meant to me that Daddy wouldn't be walking me up the aisle.

Mother addressed the minister while still comforting me. "He died two years ago. Mary Louise misses him very much. This is our first major family event without him."

"I'm terribly sorry for your loss. I didn't know— Father of the groom?"

"Here," Bert said, hopping forward, shaking his hand in the air.

"Excellent. Now let's talk about the order of the procession. Traditionally, an usher walks the mother of the bride up the aisle first, and the father of the bride walks the bride up last. Obviously, we cannot do that this time. If there is a stepfather, uncle, or other important male figure in the bride's life, he could walk her up the aisle."

"There isn't," Mother said.

"In that case, the mother of the bride could stand up and give her away," he suggested.

"No," I sobbed, "I'll walk down the aisle by myself. It'd look silly for someone to give me away at my age."

After I regained my composure, the rest of the rehearsal went off without a hitch and nothing awful happened at the dinner afterward. Bert beamed while giddy Rose gave uninformed bystanders the impression she was getting married. My family and friends ate their meals as if they were attending a wake. I was famished after having had a good cry. The prime rib was medium rare, just how I like it. I even scarfed down the delectable pecan pie.

The next morning, as Mother, Beth, and Evelyn put their finishing touches on me in the church basement, Mom said, "You still have time. You don't have to go through with this."

"Don't go there. I'm getting married and popping out a granddaughter for you."

"It's your life." She exhaled, looking disgusted with me.

When my attendants were fully satisfied they'd made me beautiful, we migrated to the lobby of the church and waited for *The Wedding March* to start. As I positioned myself to be at the end of the procession, I saw a photograph of a beautiful bride on the wall. At second glance, I realized it was a mirror. I beamed radiantly. Ollie was handsome in tails, and Evelyn looked ravishing in her red dress. I hoped it worked its magic for her.

Ollie looked at me and said, "You look gorgeous. Let's skip this and go to the hotel."

"No way. This is the price of admission."

The rest of the ceremony, photos afterward, and the reception were all a blur. Having a late flight that evening, we checked into the airport hotel to change clothes and rest a bit for the flight. Rest? Hah! Ollie literally ripped my wedding gown off me, damaging it badly. I didn't care. I wouldn't be using it again.

Coming out of a daze, I realized this was a peak sperm-count time, and I shouldn't let it go to waste. Noticing he already had my lace panties—something blue—off, I hopped up on the bed on all fours so he could take me doggy style, a position he liked, and one that was good for conception.

"Take me, Ollie. Give me the best you've got." I must have sounded pathetic, but he was lusting for me, and I was in heat. I could've said anything.

He had me quickly. I did nothing to forestall an early ejaculation. Great sex was no longer important, getting pregnant was.

As soon as Ollie finished, I flipped over on my back and slid down over the side of the bed until my shoulders rested on the floor, buttocks just above the mattress, and legs in the air, splayed as wide as I could. I pushed up with my hands until I stood on my head. I scissored my legs back and forth and bounced up and down.

"Swim, swim, swim," I shouted to encourage his sperm to fertilize my egg.

Ollie's mouth dropped wide open, probably thinking I had gone crazy. But he just stood there watching me. He got what he wanted from me—great sex with a bonus, no demands about my pleasure—and I was determined to get from him what I wanted—a daughter.

We rested in the room a couple of hours, then changed into comfortable traveling clothes and headed for the plane. I left my torn gown behind. Perhaps a maid could repair it for herself or a friend. The rest and the long flight to London gave Ollie a chance to resupply his sperm bank, but not nearly long enough to fill it to its full capacity. We landed in London in the early morning. Ollie wanted to sleep, but he wasn't nearly recharged yet, which meant I needed to keep his clothes on him.

"Ollie, you know the travel guides recommend staying up the first day to minimize jetlag," I said, forcing my eyes to stay open.

"You were so scrumptious in your wedding dress once wasn't enough last night, Nookie." He wasn't letting jetlag affect his libido and his equating me to pussy was compatible with my impregnation plan.

"Make you a deal. Let me take today off. I'll be spectacular tomorrow."

"Okay," he agreed, because I always delivered on my promises when it came to sex.

I planned on being a fucking machine until he got me pregnant or he tired of it, whichever came later. I vowed to avoid oral sex, no matter how much I desired to give it, until a baby grew within me. If he asked me for it, I'd convince him he'd enjoy coming inside me much more except when I was riding the cotton pony, something I hoped not to do again until after the baby was born. Sometimes it worked. "Waste no sperm, want not for baby" was my new motto.

I modified my sex schedule for the honeymoon, spreading my legs for Ollie whenever he wanted to plug me and not bugging him to breed except when his sperm count was highest or when I was ovulating. At those times, I insisted on maximum-possibility-of-conception positions.

When I had the energy, I put my Shanghai Squeeze to good use energizing his swimmers. Otherwise, I agreed to any fucking position he wanted whether I liked it or not. Maybe quantity of tries would make up for quality, sperm-count-wise. Ollie was pleased, to say the least. And why not? Little Ollie was getting as much exercise as he could handle, maybe more. It also made him bolder.

"Say, Nooks. You've never given me a Rusty Trombone. My frat brother told me they're awesome."

"I don't like to stick my tongue there, but tell you what. Knock me up, and I'll give you one. Give me a daughter, and you'll get another. Give me a son, you give *me* a Rusty Trumpet."

"How 'bout a preview?" He grinned like a Cheshire cat.

I stroked his bone a few times then pushed him onto his back and rode him cowgirl style.

He slapped the bed. "This isn't a preview. You're just doing me in your favorite position."

I paused in place. "No rim-jobs till I'm preggers," I said, then rode him with so much passion and enthusiasm I'd make a mink blush trying to plant his seed as deeply in me as possible.

We spent our honeymoon in London, Paris, and Geneva—four days in each, three after subtracting travel time. We did some sightseeing. I insisted on that. But he had me in the sack whenever I'd allow, and I welcomed most anything that would put his sperm in close proximity to my eggs. When I awoke to an all-day rain in London, I could see weather wouldn't permit going out and knew he'd want to stay in bed all day.

Ollie's morning wood triggered my thinking. He soon awoke to find himself in my mouth. The first encounter of the day was underway. I'd decided to put this time to use for a scientific experiment. As soon as he was wide awake, I played cowgirl, mentally recording our start time. When he came, I logged his finish time. I subtly let him know I wanted it again as soon as he could do it. "Come on, big boy, give it to me again. I'm ready." I repeated variations on this theme until I could no longer wake him from a deep sleep that night.

I recorded his recovery times and quantity of sperm—estimated, not measured—for each encounter. The numbers suggested a good way to reduce the likelihood of a birth control failure resulting in pregnancy. Giving him oral sex—multiple times even better and especially tasty after feeding him peaches or pineapple—before having intercourse reduced the quantity of sperm available to impregnate my egg. Just the opposite, sort of, strategy I employed to get pregnant. What fun I had that day! Knowing I wasn't likely to get pregnant no matter what I did or how well I did it, took the pressure off and allowed me to just play. But the next day and the rest of the trip, I worked diligently.

I delayed our morning sessions and stayed out sightseeing until dinner to avoid the temptation of afternoon delights—yet another sacrifice I made to have a baby.

Going to bed nude in hotels was now safe with a husband to protect me. Conjugating immediately after dinner maximized the sperm counts for both evening and morning inseminations. Ollie usually fell asleep immediately after the evening exercise. Some women say they feel their eggs fertilize and thus know exactly when they conceive. I didn't feel anything different. Maybe I missed it. By my calculations, if I didn't have a tampon in me by the time we touched down in New York, I would have had a successful honeymoon.

On our last full day in Geneva, our sightseeing brought us into the shopping district.

"Nookie, let's go in here," he said, after expressing boredom over having seen too many churches and historic sites to suit him.

"Okay." We walked into a store selling high-end Swiss watches, one of many luxury goods I'd studiously avoided, even since I could afford one.

"My buddies would be so envious if I had a Rolex. So would your friends." He gave me the why-don't you-try-it look, the same one he used to talk me into some sex act I thought was gross.

Letting him have one might help keep him around. I don't want to be a single parent. Hmmm. Here's an idea. "Let's buy each other one as wedding gifts." *He should like this. Mine won't cost as much as his.*

"That's a great idea." He kissed me on the cheek. "I'd like that one." He pointed to an Oyster Perpetual Datejust in stainless steel with 18 karat gold trim.

His Rolex would be worth every penny it cost me if it made him a good husband.

Our last morning in Geneva, the last day of my honeymoon, premenstrual cramps woke me. *Damn it!* I wasn't pregnant. June, July, August, and over half of September gone with no baby on the way. What was I to do?

CHAPTER 15

Having His Baby

On the long flight back to New York, I plotted a new strategy for getting pregnant to implement immediately, but the on-board restroom wasn't roomy enough for what I had in mind. I decided to bide my time reading a magazine, but I pulled the wrong one from the rack by mistake. As I was about to put the men's health monthly back, "How many ejaculations are best?" jumped off the cover at me.

Back at my seat, I read that a 2,000-year-old Chinese text named *Su Nu Jing* prescribed numbers of ejaculations per day for men of various ages to maintain proper health. However, my primary objective was to have a baby, not to make my husband live forever. We could worry about his health after I had my daughter. Becoming great with child as soon as possible was first, last and foremost in my mind.

A statistician with two degrees, such as myself, found interpolating data from the table to apply to a thirty-five-year-old mere child's play. But these numbers concerned me little because I viewed them as minimums rather the ideal. And it wouldn't hurt Ollie a bit to double my exposures when I was ovulating. There'd be plenty of time for him to rest after he knocked me up.

Energized by this new information, I drove us home to my apartment from the Newark airport but took a detour along the way.

I had started looking for a house the day after Ollie gave me the ring. Providing my daughter a stable home in a good neighborhood motivated me more than my detest of moving discouraged me. For her to have all the advantages I didn't have, good schools were essential. After walking through several houses that would've been adequate except they weren't in acceptable neighborhoods, I found one near Brainy Boro Post Office. It was perfect, a short, safe walk from the elementary school in a small suburban town known for its intelligent inhabitants, according to the Chamber of Commerce.

❧

"This isn't the way home," said Ollie who was suffering from jetlag.

"Don't you want to see if we have a home?"

"Uh, okay." He slumped into his seat, knowing it would take a lot longer to get to bed.

Several minutes later, I pulled to the curb in front of the house we'd submitted an offer on the day before our wedding.

"They must not have taken our offer," I said, feeling disappointed seeing no under-contract banner plastered on the for-sale sign.

"Huh," Ollie grunted before opening his eyes. "At least they haven't sold it to someone else."

My heart beat faster knowing the house of my dreams was still available. "We could make another offer."

"Sure. Split the difference between what we offered and the asking price." He closed his eyes.

Arriving at my apartment, I raced in, leaving Ollie to contend with the suitcases. Ignoring my desperate need to pee, I dialed the realtor, shifting my weight from foot to foot.

"The sellers rejected your bid," he said in an I-told-you-so manner.

"Did they counter offer?"

"If you call not dropping a penny a counter."

"Tell them we'll meet them halfway," I said without hiding my irritation.

"They won't take it."

"Just do it." I hung up and dashed to the bathroom, fearful I wouldn't make it.

Emerging from nature's call, I noticed the chaos that had formerly been my tidy little apartment. Ollie's buddies had moved his things in before taking him to his bachelor party the evening before our wedding. I had never before dealt with this much stuff crowded into such a small space.

Sharing the digs that had been all mine for several

years, and after having lived alone—mostly—since I was nineteen caused me to feel cramped. Adapting to a man sharing my bathroom who had different attitudes toward hygiene challenged me. I dealt with the situation by spending as much time as humanly possible in bed.

Two days later, the realtor called to tell us the seller had accepted our offer. His somber voice suggested that he was disappointed in getting a smaller commission than he'd anticipated. The sellers asked for two months to close to give them time to move into the place they were buying. I spent my out-of-work time picking out drapes, carpeting and, most importantly, furnishings for my daughter's room. After bouncing my bedsprings relentlessly, they gave out. I added a box spring and mattress set to the list. No way did I want my little girl to hear her mother having sex.

 споса

That I had my period—again—after we moved into our very own house pissed me off. I'm not normally terribly irritable, but Ollie wasn't getting the job done, and each onset of premenstrual cramps painfully reminded me of his failure. It was simple for me to understand, if I bled I was healthy and ready to be called Mama.

I stormed out of the bathroom and shook my package of tampons in his face, shouting, "You're a fucking failure."

He turned away. "Or do you mean a failure at fucking?"

"Both!" I felt ashamed. It wasn't necessarily his fault. My eggs may have passed their expiration date.

I loved our house, especially making it my nest. It had more rooms and a lot more space than any house I'd ever lived in before. Decorating my daughter's room was so exciting. I made it the bedroom I had always wanted to have as a girl. It was ready for her when I got pregnant, if that should ever happen.

With no point in having intercourse during my period, I gave him oral sex. My oral sex is always good, but my make-up oral sex is superb, even better when I'm at fault for starting the fight. Maybe Ollie figured that out and intentionally provoked me during my periods. He might have been that devious. I could be as sharp with him as I was at my worst with other men. Ollie's insensitivity helped. He was unfazed where Tim would have been crushed because, like me, he was highly sensitive.

Drugstores wouldn't sell me home pregnancy tests by the dozen, so I ordered a gross of my company's The Rabbit Died product, supposedly for a study I was running. Any morning I woke with the slightest chance of having a pea in my pod, I pissed on a strip. No luck. When I was down to only a dozen, I ordered another gross.

One cold March Monday, I got a different result in my early morning test. "It's pink! It's pink! Ollie, look!" *Pink might be a sign she's going to be a girl.* I ran through the house to show him the good news, but he wasn't there.

Damn! I'd forgotten that he'd planned on going into

work early that day. I picked up the phone and dialed.

"Tookie here. I need a favor. A special favor." Seeing my reflection in the window, I thought I must look strange to the neighbors, talking on the phone naked as night.

"I owe you several," said Marge in the lab at work.

"I'll be right there. I need you to run that new, super-accurate pregnancy blood test."

"You're not!"

I turned to look at my profile in the reflection to see if I showed yet.

"I hope I am." In my haste, I mistakenly threw on my pink-spattered painting clothes and raced to work, where I dashed directly to the lab.

Marge grinned from ear to ear when she saw my disheveled mess fly through the door.

"Sit there," she said, pointing to a chair with two padded arms.

I plopped down, feet and legs too excited to keep still.

"Which arm?"

Which arm? How the hell do I know which arm? I'm right handed. Does that mean I should have her use my left arm?

"Which arm did they take blood from for your blood test?"

"What blood test?" I couldn't think.

"For your marriage license, silly."

"My left. No, my right. No, I don't remember. Just hurry."

Marge rubbed the inside of one elbow, then the other. "There's a nice vein in your left one. Make a fist." She thumped the vein to make it easier to stab.

Before I knew it, she'd sucked a quart of blood out of me and covered the hole with a Band-Aid.

"Get to work. I'll call you as soon as I have the results." She pushed me toward the door. "A watched centrifuge never settles."

I didn't get much work done that day. Most of it I spent thinking about how great my life would be when Lara arrived. But what if this pink pee strip was just a false positive? When my phone rang around three, I just knew it was THE call.

"You're gonna need a new wardrobe, Tooks!"

"Thank you! Thank you! Thank you! If there's anything I can ever do for you, just ask. Would you like to be Lara's godmother?"

I'd never been so excited or indescribably happy in my life. I called Rose to share my joy.

"Bert, I've got some news to tell Rose."

He must not have put his hand over the phone when he informed her. "Rose, Tookie has somedink to tell you. She sounds excited." *Clomp, clomp, clomp, clomp. Clomp.*

"Vat good news do you have for me?" she said, sounding short of breath.

"I tested positive this morning."

"A baby is on his vay?" She sounded just as excited as I was.

"Yes! She'll be here late November or December."

"Vat does Oliver dink?" Rose sounded concerned about her son's reaction to him becoming a father.

"He doesn't know yet. Don't call or come over tonight. We'll be celebrating." I said with as friendly a voice as I could muster so as not to aggravate her.

Rather than calling Ollie at work, I decided to wait to tell him in person. On the way home, I bought the first two maternity dresses I found in my size.

When I heard his car pull into the driveway, I picked up the plastic trombone kazoo bought months ago for just this occasion and greeted him at the door playing it.

"You all right?" Somehow he found a way to arch his eyebrows over his saucered eyes.

"What makes you say that, big boy?" I said in my pathetic Dietrich impersonation.

"It's March, you don't have a stitch on, and you're playing a trombone kazoo. What could be unusual about that?" He looked as if he thought he'd have to have me committed.

"It's you who's out of step. Take your clothes off now, and get into the shower."

Finally, the light came on. "Y—You're pregnant!" I couldn't tell if he was relieved I wasn't crazy or afraid of the responsibilities of becoming a father.

"You bet your bippie I am. The rabbit died." I would've done cartwheels if I could. "Move it." I slapped his butt. "Get yourself naked right now, or I'll rip that new silk shirt off you."

Seeing that I was about to make good on my promise to give him a Rusty Trombone, he had his clothes off and was in the tub in an instant. After setting a world record for fewest seconds spent in a shower, he emerged dripping wet.

"Dry off first." I couldn't recall Ollie ever being as impatient for anything I did for him. "Don't forget, you promised to reciprocate if it's not a girl."

Not wanting to have my tongue there any longer than absolutely necessary, I rubbed my love brush against his impregnator to get him even more aroused. He responded quite well, as usual. I dropped to my knees to start sucking. "You know I love it when you do that, but you promised—"

"I'm just warming you up. Didn't you play scales on your trumpet before your band concerts?"

"Yeees, but I've been looking forward to this for so long."

"Have a little patience for once."

When he could no longer keep his heels flat on the floor, I knew from experience he was tuned up and spun him around, facing him toward the tub. A little tap on his inner thigh signaled him to spread his legs wide. After a couple of licks and a few strokes, his trombone messed the shower curtain.

"Wow! Will you give me another one later?"

"When I return from the hospital with my daughter. Now, I have something waiting for you in the guest bedroom.

He looked like we had landed on Mars when he walked through the doorway. "Why's a sheet of plastic covering the bed?"

"You'll see in good time. Lie down."

He apparently didn't notice the chocolate syrup and whipped cream on the nightstand. I smeared chocolate sauce on his abdomen, inner thighs, and on my favorite places. I got him ready again by nibbling on him as I licked off the chocolate. Afterward, he collapsed on the bed. You'd think he was the one who had done all the work.

In a glassy-eyed stupor, he said, "I don't know if I just had the time of my life or narrowly escaped death from a mad woman."

"Take your choice." I was energized and ready for more, wanting to celebrate this happiest day of my life. "What do you want me to do for you now?"

"Nookie, I don't think I'm man enough for you."

"You're man enough to knock me up, you brute." I pounced on him and started kissing him.

I loved being pregnant so much I started wearing maternity clothing as soon as I missed my second period, months before I showed. My being with child pleased Ollie, as well. I no longer badgered him about having sex this way or that or when to or when not to have it. He could have it any time or any way he wanted—when I wasn't in the bathroom throwing up. I let him have all the fun and didn't pester him about having an orgasm or even to watch me diddle myself.

On those occasions I needed to climax, Sydney took care of me. Being so contented because my baby was on her way, he was needed so seldom I sometimes forgot to keep fresh batteries on hand. I let Ollie be as selfish as only he could because I had what I wanted.

Needing more sleep now required me to go to bed earlier than him, resulting in me falling asleep before he came to bed. But one night after we had been out for a movie, he finally noticed my tits had expanded to B cups when I emerged from our bathroom naked.

His lascivious look told me something was going on in his dirty little mind. His brown eyes followed my chest on its route from the bathroom to the light switch and then, I suppose, to the bed to lie down.

As soon as my skin touched the sheet, his hand began stroking my thigh. "Roll onto your back."

Assuming he was about to mount me, I spread my legs wide.

"I want to do something new tonight," he said as he pushed them together. Straddling me, he bent over to suck Lucy before titillating Ethel's nipple with his tongue. With both fully erect, he flopped his head back and forth between them humming something unintelligible as he did it.

It all seemed strange to me but, as I felt his erection poke my thigh, I realized my funbags would keep him entertained at least until our daughter was born and while she was nursing. Right then I decided to extend that as long as possible, maybe till kindergarten.

When Ollie tired of motorboating me, he moved forward, sliding his pulsing desire along my stomach and up my chest. No man had ever done that before. He grasped my wrists to pull my hands up to the outsides of my breasts.

When they were where he wanted them, he said, "Push them together."

"You like my new…uh… dimensions?"

"Oh, yeah," he responded in his poor Barry White imitation.

I adjusted the pressure against his prick as he humped my tits wildly, another new experience for a formerly bustless woman. A bonus was how much feeling him rub against the sides of my breasts excited me.

Ollie started tensing up.

Oh shit. He's gonna mess all over me. "I want you now."

Ollie tried to shift his body down mine, but I resisted.

"No. Here." I pulled him to my mouth for a bonus.

He happily obliged me with a double dollop of my favorite protein and eliminated the need to shower.

I slept especially contentedly that night knowing he had found more reasons to hang around.

✺

What a time he had with my new toys. I enjoyed his playing with my Dagmars, as he had started calling them, because he hadn't always given them enough attention to suit me. But they were awkward, hanging out in front of me, bouncing all over the place, changing my center of balance.

I wondered why some women had theirs enlarged. If they had any sense, they'd have them reduced to the smallest size possible and inflate them when they wanted to attract men or have sex.

In the middle of my third month, the obstetrician ordered an amniocentesis to check for genetic abnormalities often found in older mothers. She warned me about the pain, but not the worst part. She needed my bladder overly full for some strange reason and had me drink something like twenty gallons of water right before the test. To make matters worse, my bladder had to stay full the duration of the test, which ran much longer than expected due to some technical problem with her equipment. I was about to run naked through the waiting room to relieve myself when she mercifully finished the test and directed me to a restroom two doors down the hall. I raced to it with my ass hanging out the back of that useless piece of cloth hospitals force patients to wear.

I detested the test and feared what the results might be but, after two days, I got a call.

"Good news! You're going to have a normal baby boy."

"A boy?"

"That's right. A healthy baby boy."

CHAPTER 16

Rose's Delight

Shocked by the news, a million things ran through my brain. Rose would be thrilled. After going this far, I wouldn't have another abortion. I might not get pregnant again. I'd carry him to term. Maybe, if I was lucky, someone would switch babies in the hospital, and I would get my girl.

One thing was clear. I was going to try again. I was going to have a daughter if it killed me. That was all there was to it.

As my belly got larger and larger, household tasks that required bending or squatting became daunting.

"You've outdone yourself this time," I said to Ollie at the dinner table after he had prepared a new dish. "But I need some help around here."

"I work, and I cook," he responded.

"You do both of them very well, but I work, and I clean the house, and I do the laundry, take out the gar-bage, do the dishes, go shopping, pay the bills, have the cars serviced, coordinate the repairmen, and do our taxes. There's probably more."

"Hire a cleaning woman. We can afford one—What's on TV tonight?"

"I can't imagine having a strange person in our house, especially a servant." A shiver ran up my spine just thinking about having a maid picking through my things.

"She wouldn't even be an employee. You'd be paying for a service, like a plumber." He left the room to watch golf on TV.

Unconvinced having someone poking around wouldn't be intrusive, I continued doing everything like before. I set all other emotions aside, focusing all my attention on having this baby. The sooner I had him, the sooner I could get to work on getting pregnant with my daughter.

The closer to delivery I got, the more difficult doing routine housework became. In my ninth month, I had to live with my house not being as clean as I liked. One early December morning, I struggled to mop the kitchen floor.

Damn. I had to pee in the worst way but thought I could hold it, because I was almost finished. *Whoosh. Better start doing Kegels again. Oh, oh! That's not pee. Owww! That's not a cramp. It's a contraction. Better hurry. Don't want to leave the floor a mess.*

After the linoleum was spic and span, I called Rose.

"Can you send Bert over? It's time." *Oww. Another contraction.*

Sounding like she'd just won the lottery, Rose said, "I'll come, too. He doesn't know anydink about havink babies."

"Give me a few minutes to clean up." I didn't want the doctor and nurses to see me looking like I'd wet myself.

With a firm voice, she said, "Just get your bag. Ve're comink now," and hung up.

With so much to attend to, I left calling Ollie to them.

My labor was relatively easy, especially for a first-time mom. Somehow exposing myself to half the town didn't give me the kick I'd hoped it would in my carefree days. The delivery room crew didn't seem to get much out of seeing everything I've got, either.

I didn't see my baby immediately after he was born. They supposedly carried him away to weigh, measure, and clean him.

I wondered if they weren't bringing him to me because they knew I wanted a girl and thought I might do something rash.

The nurse interrupted my thoughts. "Here's your beautiful baby boy." She pulled back the sheet and placed him ever so carefully on my naked chest.

She's just saying that because she knows I'm unhappy. I counted his fingers and toes and stroked his hair.

"You're right. He is beautiful. I've never seen such a beautiful baby."

"See if he'll suckle." She helped position him on Lucy, but he cried.

"He hates me," I said, feeling guilty for not wanting him.

"Nothing of the sort. Some babies have a preference." She shifted him gently to Ethel, from whom he fed voraciously.

"Make sure he drains that one before you shift him to the other one. Your most nutritious milk is at the bottom." She pulled the sheet over us, leaving his little head exposed, and left.

He had curly red hair and was opinionated, almost from birth. His preference for Ethel over Lucy was just the start. He got worse as he got older. However, it was love at first sight.

I'd selected a girl's name ages before getting pregnant, but hadn't come up with something for a boy. I'd always found the actor, Jeremy Irons, to be darkly handsome.

"Ollie, what do you think about naming him Jeremy?" I said, showing him my baby for the first time.

"Aren't we going to name him Junior, after me?"

I shook my head vigorously. "And not Bert and not my father's or brothers' names either. I'm gonna name him Jeremy."

"Okay. I'll call him Jere for short." Ollie acquiesced like he usually did when I insisted on something—provided it didn't require him to do anything. Rose didn't care. I could've named him Dweezil. All she wanted was a healthy, handsome grandson, and I gave her one.

୧৩୧৩

My mother caught the last flight of the day out of Memphis, the cheapest one available, arriving at eleven-something at night, to be with me when I came home from the hospital. Ollie grumbled about having to pick her up so late but was there when she trotted out of the jetway. She was a great help because I hadn't cared for an infant since my youngest brother was born twenty-five years earlier.

Mother would rise early and scoop up Jere as soon as he finished his first feeding of the morning. She'd burp him and clean him up and change his diaper and tend to his every whim while I got to rest. By the time Rose arrived, he'd be sleeping again. Mother's greediness caused trouble with Rose, who felt that her time with her grandson had been usurped.

My mother-in-law, grumpy at being deprived of time with her grandson, would make breakfast for the four of us and get Ollie off to work. Although Mother and Rose didn't get along, they made my life the weeks after delivering Jere much easier.

Ollie's life changed little. He golfed as much as when he was single and hung out with his buddies when he felt like it. The one thing he did around the house was something I hated to do—cook. That part of my marriage worked well.

I didn't repaint the baby's room. I just converted another bedroom for the boy baby, painted it blue, and furnished it accordingly. The pink room waited, ready for my future daughter.

After my mother returned to Arkansas, I was finally

alone with Jere. That nickname and his sperm were Ollie's only contributions to his son. Just the two of us by ourselves. It was heaven. Two days after my mother left, Rose appeared on my doorstep smiling like a Cheshire cat. I hoped she wouldn't make a habit of dropping by like this. I needed my alone time to recharge while the baby rested.

"Jeremy's asleep," I said, eyelids dropping so she might take the hint and leave.

"I've got a gift for you, a very special gift." She grinned even broader than before, if that was possible.

"That's nice." I thought she had brought some sort of trinket or clothing for the new baby.

"I don't dink you understand just how special this gift is." She tried to look mysterious by hushing her voice. "Here's a hint. Carver-Vatkins."

Jere's closet was full of the C-W products I needed. Girlfriends from there had loaded me up at my shower.

She took me by the hand and led me into the living room.

"Here, sit down." She pointed to the wing chair by the fireplace and perched on the edge of the raised hearth.

"Don't you want to see the baby?" I asked to break the eerie mood.

She shook her head. "Not just yet."

This was odd. Rose always wanted to see Jere and play with him. He was the apple of her eye.

"Dear, I have a gift for you dat Jere should never see." Rose was more serious, even when she had confronted me about my past.

"O—Okay?" I was stumped.

She handed me a videotape. A typed label read, "Carver-Watkins Security," followed by a smudged penciled-in date.

I sank into the chair, hiding my face from Rose behind the wing. "Is this what I think it is?"

"Yes," she said, as serious as an inquisitor.

"Have you seen it?" *Please say you haven't.*

"I envy you. I never had the guts."

I took the tape cassette out of the cardboard sleeve and scrutinized it closely while my stomach churned wildly.

"Put it into your VCR." She nudged me toward the TV.

"Why?" I really didn't want her to see this. Who knows what they caught me doing?

"I need you to verify dat this is de right tape and de only time you vere taped."

When it started to play, I saw myself walking across the Carver-Watkins parking lot wearing my hippy office-sex dress. It could've been worse. They didn't film me doing anybody. I just exposed myself to the guards.

"I threw that dress into the dumpster when I quit Carver-Watkins." I felt ashamed that she had seen my attempt at being an exhibitionist.

I didn't realize what good resolution the security cameras had. Everything was distinct. Even putting on thin white panties hadn't blocked out much. Thank God it wasn't in color.

"Rose—" I blubbered incoherently. I would've joked

about this before Jere was born, but everything was different after he arrived.

"Vat's important is dat your kids never see dis. Oliver vould dink it's cool, but no child should ever see his moder like dis." She looked more sad than angry.

"Does Ollie know about this?" He'd watch it over and over and tease me about it. The kids might walk in. He might even leave it lying around for them to find.

"Of course not. Do you dink I'm a fool?" She gave me the evil eye.

"Bert?" I was less worried about him because Rose hadn't told him anything about my past.

"He doesn't need to know you did dose dings."

I tasted vomit coming up my throat. "Don't they record over those tapes?"

"Not juicy ones like dis." She shook her head.

"I guess they wouldn't. Do the guards have others?" A chill ran down my spine.

"Uder days or uder copies?" She focused her eyes on the tape without blinking.

"Other copies. There were no other days." My C-W escapades ran across my memory. Lots of office sex, but nothing in view of security cameras—I hoped.

"I offered dem so much, dey vould've sold dem to me if dey had dem."

"How'd you get it?" I shook with fear as I waited for her answer.

"Don't vorry about dat." Apparently satisfied, Rose became nonchalant.

"How can I repay you?"

"You be de vorld's best moder to my grandchildren and as good a vife to my son as you can."

"That's all?" I didn't know whether I should feel relieved or not.

"Dat's vat'll make me happy."

I cried as I hugged her.

"Hand me de tape." Standing by the fireplace, she said, "Give me some lighter fluid." She doused the tape and tossed it into the fireplace. "You can have de honor."

I threw in a lighted match, starting a blaze.

"Any photos of you naked or havink sex?"

"I wasn't that stupid. I wouldn't have pulled that stunt if I'd known they had videotape machines back then."

"Dank God for dat."

We watched the fire melt the tape into an unrecognizable glob of black plastic.

Rose smiled and patted my back. "Let me see Jere now."

I loved being alone at home with Jeremy. Breastfeeding him was the high point of my day. I loved how it felt when he suckled. I also loved feeling his warmth against me. One advantage of tiny breasts is the smaller amount of milk they hold when full. Jeremy got less nourishment per feeding from me than he would have from an average-sized mother. So, I had the pleasure of nursing him more often. I loved my little breasts even more because they gave me more reasons to hold Jeremy close to me.

I always breastfed in complete privacy, even if it meant retreating to a bedroom when visitors were in the house. Jeremy was more relaxed and ate better when we were alone, even better in a darkened room.

Another reason I breastfed in privacy was that I often became aroused sexually, even to the point of having an orgasm a few times. That was a shock as climaxes don't come easily for me. Just ask my boyfriends about that.

Getting aroused during breastfeeding had a very positive side to it. After being very pleasantly shocked by the first one, I read an article—one of the advantages of working for big Pharma was having ready access to all the good health-related publications—that discussed this very issue. As it turns out, I—being special as always—was among a small minority of women who sometimes had an orgasm while breastfeeding with no stimulation other than the baby's suckling.

Mother and Rose both cautioned me about losing the desire for sex. "If you want to keep your husband around, you must tend to his needs, too, not just the baby's." I stumbled onto a ready solution one night.

Aroused from breastfeeding, I slipped into the bed quietly, in the dark to find Ollie already there.

"Speaking of Nookie, I haven't had much lately."

I slid down and suckled Ollie first to full arousal and then for my pleasure. Problem solved. I needed him, not only to provide for Jeremy but to give me a daughter. I wasn't about to give up on having a girl after just one try.

Although I loved being alone with Jeremy, he wasn't an easy baby. Perhaps he sensed the lack of his father's love. Sometimes, he would cry just for the sake of crying when he wasn't wet or hungry and didn't want to be held.

On one particular day, I had work to do at home and couldn't quiet him. Nothing worked. There was nothing wrong with him. It was as if he was punishing me. After an hour of his screaming, I became so frustrated, I banged my hand on the table so hard, I hurt it. I never, ever, would hit my child. I'd kill myself first.

I needed intellectual stimulation being alone with a baby twenty-four/seven didn't give me. So, I returned to work full-time in the spring of 1987. Juggling working full-time, caring for a baby, and managing a household exhausted me. It apparently showed, not to Ollie, but to his parents. One Friday, Rose cooked a nice meal and brought it over to us so I could relax that evening, with no pots and pans to scrub. I was grateful. Sitting around the table after the meal was over, we had a discussion.

"Oliver, your moder noticed how tired and frazzled Tookie is after returning to vork," Bert said calmly.

Ollie flipped through a golf magazine, unconcerned. "I hadn't noticed much difference."

"You vouldn't," interjected Rose with a sharper tone than I'd heard her use with Ollie before.

I didn't want to do anything to rock the boat, even though I was floundering. "I can manage."

"Shush," Rose said, as she patted my hand.

"So, Rose and I decided to do somedink about it." Bert handed me a check.

My jaw dropped. I couldn't believe my eyes. I choked out, "There must be a mistake. This is an enormous amount of money." I handed it to Ollie.

"This is as much as our mortgage. We can't accept this," Ollie said.

Bert stood and lectured his son. "You vill accept it, and you vill use it to pay off your mortgage, so Tookie von't have to kill herself goink to vork."

"Do you really mean it?" I asked, crying with relief.

"Of course ve do," Rose said. "A better daughter-in-law and a more beautiful grandson, I couldn't have."

"Handsome," Bert interjected.

"How can we ever repay you?" I asked, trembling.

"By beink good parents and stayink togeder. Ve don't vant our grandchildren comink from a broken home," said Rose.

"Grand*children?*" Ollie almost panicked.

"I'm not pregnant," I stated. "Yet."

"You vill be, and ve vant you to be. Rose tells me you vant a daughter more than anythink in the vorld," Bert said.

"Ve vant you to have her. Our grandson needs a playmate and to learn how to share," said Rose. "Ve also expect our son to be a better husband and father." Rose shot daggers in Ollie's direction.

Tears streamed down my face as I hugged and thanked them.

I switched from full to part-time to spend more time with Jeremy. I loved being with him, but I also enjoyed having adult conversations at work. I never had any at home. Rose and Bert understood my need to work. They supported me by providing daycare for Jeremy the two days a week I worked out of the house. They didn't want strangers caring for their grandson. This arrangement worked perfectly to everyone's satisfaction. Peace and harmony reigned in both households.

I was still single in most respects but without the perks. I managed the household, paid all the bills, filed our taxes, shopped for groceries, washed the clothes, scheduled doctors' appointments, and coordinated repairs and deliveries. You name it, I did it.

But Ollie continued to live his bachelor life, except I was the one doing everything for him instead of his mother. I didn't mind because I had Jeremy. He made being married palatable. I spent as much time with him as I could. When I wasn't at work, I had Jeremy with me running errands, cleaning the house. Wherever I was, he was.

When he was nineteen months old, I turned thirty-eight, and my biological clock clanged as loudly as if Big Ben was in the next room. I had to get my crack cracking if I was going to have a daughter. I'd be thirty-nine when she would be born if Ollie only took three months to knock me up. I refused to think how old I'd be if he took longer. I saw no need to bother him, so I quietly put a plan in place. No more sponges or oral sex now that I wanted to be fertile again. Birth control had kept me from getting pregnant again too soon. No way could I manage two children in diapers at the same time. I might have put too much pressure on Ollie to perform before, so I didn't burden him this time.

Spreading out our encounters to maximize his sperm count wasn't an issue this time. He still liked sex with me, although not as often or as intensely, but responded well enough when I initiated things. But he seldom jumped me unexpectedly anymore. He never was affectionate outside the bedroom. That didn't change.

I gave myself the best chance by having him every day I was ovulating. I mounted him much more often than in our recent history, but not so much he suspected anything. This approach provided better results than the scheme used for my first implantation, and it was much less stressful for him. So stress-free was he, my announcement came as a complete surprise.

"I—I th—thought you used birth control." Beads of sweat appeared on his forehead.

"I quit. I'm too old to wait any longer." It wasn't like my wanting a girl was any big surprise.

He wiped his face with his handkerchief. "When are you due?

"*She*'s due in late November." *I'll soon be needing my hatching jackets. Better see if they still fit.*

"She? That's only five months away! Why didn't you tell me before?" He grabbed his head with both hands.

"I wanted to make sure. I was afraid I'd miscarry." That was the truth. I had a deathly fear of losing this baby.

"What'll Mother and Dad say?" Now, he looked worried his parents would disapprove.

"They're thrilled." Rose and Bert were my strongest allies.

He actually looked surprised. "You told them already?"

"Of course. They're interested."

"Should I shower first?" He got the look on his face he got when he knew I was about to give him extraordinary sex.

"If you want. But don't expect anything fancy from me. You reneged last time. I'm not exactly in the mood to give you anything just now."

ဆာ

I enjoyed my second pregnancy much more than the first. It was much easier physically and emotionally because I knew what to expect. Ollie wouldn't leave me for getting pregnant again. I made his life too comfortable. Besides that, he'd never lived on his own and was afraid to try. Also, a second child required no more effort on his part than the first. None. His parents and I did everything. He did what he wanted. From his perspective, he had the perfect marriage.

Not fearing birth defects after having carried one healthy baby, I forewent the amniocentesis and convinced myself I'd accept whatever baby came. I knew I wouldn't be having any more kids, so I just hoped for the best. I didn't, however, pick out a boy's name. I stayed with the girl's name I decided upon as a teenager after seeing *Dr. Zhivago* with Tim.

Labor went easier this time. And I had my girl. While waiting for a nurse to bring Lara to me, I realized that Jere had never been alone with his father before. I wondered how he was handling it. I hoped he wasn't too stressed. *I'll have to give him special attention so he's not jealous of his sister.*

Footsteps coming into my room interrupted my reverie. "Here's your beautiful baby." The nurse handed me a tiny squiggly package wrapped in a baby blanket.

Wanting to be sure my prayers had been answered, I unwrapped my little bundle of love. *Red hair. This must be my baby for sure. It looks like a girl's face. Kinda like mine. Don't be afraid. Pull back the rest of the blanket.* "It *is* a girl! It's my Lara." I kissed her all over. She was a miniature me, but prettier. I counted the fingers and toes on her perfectly-formed hands and feet. "Thank you. She's perfect." Tim sent me flowers, but Ollie gave me Lara. I made the right choice. My life was complete. Almost.

THE END

About the Author

After a career of chasing, and being chased by, spies and assorted thugs across national monuments while being mistaken for Cary Grant, George Kaplan pawned his shoulder holster and used the money to buy a computer to serve as his word processor. Although well versed in writing after-action summaries, Kaplan had no experience with writing fiction, other than his expense reports. Government repercussions about modeling characters after his cohorts and enemies would have been far too risky, so he fabricated a heroine who has qualities he's seen a few of on each of a number of women he'd rubbed shoulders (and sometimes more) with, during his long career undercover. Kaplan's first novel, *Only Tim Sent Flowers*, launched his Tookie series about an undiagnosed Aspie girl who comes of age in the late-1960s sexual revolution. *Finding Mr. Wrong* follows his heroine on her quest for a husband and daughter.